# Cat's Prey

Other books by Dorothy Eden
in Thorndike Large Print

AN IMPORTANT FAMILY
CROW HOLLOW

# Cat's Prey

## DOROTHY EDEN

Thorndike Press • Thorndike, Maine

**Library of Congress Cataloging in Publication Data:**

Eden, Dorothy, 1912-1982.
  Cat's prey.

  1. Large type books. I. Title.
[PR9639.3.E38C3  1985]      823      84-24094
ISBN 0-89621-598-9

Large Print edition available through arrangement with
Harold Ober Associates, Inc.

Cover design by Ralph Lizotte.

# Cat's Prey

# I

Antonia knew the two letters, Iris's and Simon's, by heart. She had re-read them a dozen times before leaving London, and now the rhythm of the plane's engines and the curious unreality of fatigue was making her repeat them senselessly in her head. Over and over her mind kept saying:

*I particularly want you, dear, and so does Simon.*

Simon was her cousin. She hadn't seen him for several years. She remembered him as a fat boy with puffy eyelids, a flat shapeless nose and a good-natured grin. He used to have a passionate enthusiasm for frogs and guinea-pigs. She was surprised that he should even remember her, quite apart from wanting her to

7

come to his wedding. But of course there was that business about Aunt Laura's death too. Globe-trotting Laura, the family had always called her. Antonia couldn't remember her at all. She was her mother's eldest sister and had spent her life in unlikely places like Mexico or Peru or Persia or the South Sea Islands. To Antonia she was a letter bearing interesting foreign stamps every Christmas. She had brought one of her letters with her, as a means of establishing her identity. Because Simon had said that he and she were Aunt Laura's sole beneficiaries. The poor old dear couldn't have had much money left after her globe-trotting, but there was enough, apparently, for Simon to buy an hotel and to pay her passage by air from England.

"I've bought an hotel and I'm being married," his letter had said. "I came to New Zealand a few months ago when old Aunt Laura (do you remember her?) sent for me because she was dying. She's made me her trustee and she's left you and me her bit – you because she said your mother was her favourite sister, and me because I'm the only male in the family.

"I came out because I wasn't doing anything much else at the time, and now Iris wants this hotel (it's only a small holiday place), and we thought you might like to be in on it. Anyway,

Iris wants to meet some of my family.

"I can't start to tell you what Iris is like. I'm no good at that sort of thing. But I'm plain crazy about her. I feel like that old joker in the Bible, you know, the one who says 'Sweet is thy voice and fair is thy face.'

"I do hope you'll come, Tonia, because I want to show Iris off to someone."

That was Simon exactly as she remembered him, naïve, slow, self-effacing, absorbed in his hobbies, unable to believe anyone would ever see anything in him. One would have known that when he fell in love it would be in the worshipping way, which was dangerous as well as uncomfortable. For what woman could stay permanently on a pedestal? Iris, of course, might have that gift, for she didn't sound simple. Antonia didn't know why she had that instinct about her after just reading her letter which was very sweet, friendly and sincere.

"Simon says you're his favourite cousin and I would so much like to have you at our wedding. I know it's an awfully long way to come and we don't know what your personal circumstances are. But I am sure you would find it worth while if you could. You would like New Zealand and besides there's this business about your aunt's estate. I believe your being here would facilitate matters although Dougal

Conroy, our solicitor (he's a dear, but *so* cautious), says it isn't necessary. But quite apart from business we want you at our wedding. You don't need to worry about money because Simon and I have bought an hotel — it's just a small guesthouse, really — on a hilltop overlooking the most glorious sea, and there would be a home there for you. The place is badly in need of renovation, but we plan to spend the winter repairing it and doing up the garden, and in the summer, in its miniature way, it will be wonderful.

"Simon is sweet! I'm so madly happy I must have someone to share it with. Please do come."

Antonia had the instinctive feeling, on first reading that letter, that Iris had had very little in her life, otherwise how could she be so excited about what sounded like nothing but a glorified boarding house (and tumble-down at that), and phlegmatic old Simon. But perhaps Simon had improved a lot in the last five years, especially since he was moved to quote the Song of Solomon. Perhaps Iris really did love him. Perhaps her letter was completely sincere.

"Tea, Miss Webb?" said the stewardess, breaking into Antonia's thoughts.

"Yes, please. How long before we land?"

"About an hour. You'll be glad to get there."

Antonia stretched her weary limbs.

"I certainly will."

"It's a long trip from England the first time." The stewardess was friendly, pretty, smart in her uniform. "It makes London seem a long way away."

"London on a wet February day," said Antonia dreamily. "That was how I left it. I was glad it was raining. It didn't make me feel so homesick."

She had been homesick, of course — for her tiny flat in South Kensington, her kindly garrulous landlady, her cat curled up indifferently in his favourite spot on the window ledge (the next tenant was taking him over), the people at the office, even the rain pouring on the gulls'-wing grey London roof-tops. But there was something of the globe-trotting Aunt Laura in her. She reached out for new experiences. She couldn't resist this challenge, for she felt that that was the unwritten part of Aunt Laura's will. When, almost at the last minute, she had had a bad attack of flu and had had to postpone her reservations for a fortnight she had been consumed with impatience, and only sheer weakness had prevented her from catching the plane.

"You'll enjoy the New Zealand sunshine," said the stewardess. "What are you going to do there?"

"I don't quite know. I worked on a little weekly in London. They want me to do articles for that. But I'm going chiefly because of an inheritance."

"My goodness! You might be an heiress!"

Antonia laughed. A new land was approaching, excitement was stirring in her. Good old Aunt Laura with her legacy of travel, if nothing else. She answered the pretty stewardess.

"In the language of my Cockney friends, not bloomin' likely!"

Simon had cabled that he had reserved her a room at the Grand Hotel in Auckland. He and Iris lived at a beach suburb of Christchurch in the South Island. Antonia was to fly down in the morning. Between now and then she had sixteen hours in which to sleep. She needed them all. After the five days in a plane with the brief hours of rest at airports she was in a queer unreal dream. The clear brilliant New Zealand sky, the houses slanting up the hillsides, the little white-sailed yachts sprinkled over the shining harbour seemed nothing more than an illustration out of a travel magazine. Tomorrow she would appreciate it. Today she must sleep.

As soon as she arrived she took a hot bath and tumbled into bed. But before sleep had finally claimed her the telephone at her bedside rang. Antonia wearily roused herself. Who would this be? Simon ringing from the South Island?

"Hullo," she said drowsily.

"Is that Miss Webb?" came a man's voice, thick, a little hurried. She had the odd impression that her caller was looking over his shoulder as he spoke.

"Yes," she answered. That wasn't Simon's voice. True, she hadn't heard it for five years, but she remembered Simon's lazy enunciation, with his pronounced English accent.

"You won't know who I am," the voice went on, "but I have a little information about your aunt's death if you care to have it."

Her tiredness, pressing on her like a fog, made her unable to think. Was she asleep or was this happening in reality?

"Information? About Aunt Laura? What do you mean?"

"If you'll meet me I'll explain."

"But I don't know who you are. Why can't you tell me what you have to now?"

"Over the telephone? That wouldn't be – quite convenient."

Suddenly Antonia had a disturbing feeling of being very much alone in a strange country. Whose was this strange, heavy, slightly sinister voice? What had he to tell her about Aunt

13

Laura? If there should be trouble to whom could she turn? Not to Simon with his remembered stupidity, not to Iris with her gushing sweetness. Instinctively she knew that.

She opened her mouth to speak and knew that her voice would tremble. Fiercely she said to herself, "Pull yourself together. Act sensibly. This is nothing more than someone wanting to make a little money out of something he imagines he did for Aunt Laura. Poor old Aunt Laura. She didn't let strange countries frighten her."

"Are you there?" came the voice, as if its owner were watching her indecision with triumph.

"Yes," she said firmly. "What do you want me to do?"

"Meet me at the restaurant called Toby's at the lower end of Queen Street in half an hour."

"But I don't know you. Are you going to wear a red carnation in your buttonhole?"

"I shall know you, Miss Webb. I shall speak to you first."

How should he know her? she wondered. Had he watched her get off the plane or followed her to the hotel? Suddenly she was quite definitely disturbed and uneasy.

"Look—" she began.

"Are you frightened, Miss Webb?" came the

14

thick voice. "I assure you there's no need to be."

"Of course I'm not frightened. How absurd! But I'm very tired. Is this information important?"

"It's something you should know before you go to Christchurch."

Antonia drew a deep breath. How did he know she was going to Christchurch? No, she wouldn't start worrying about that.

"Very well. I'll meet you at four o'clock."

She was so tired. It was only the thought of Aunt Laura, who must have encountered and overcome numerous obstacles in her journeyings, or rather Aunt Laura's tough travel-worn ghost, that got her dressed and out into the bright sunshine. It was mid-afternoon and the street that ran down the hill to the little forest of masts in the harbour and the glittering bay was crowded with people. If she hadn't been so tired and so oppressed with this curious errand she would have been intensely interested in her first glimpse of a New Zealand city. She got on a tram that seemed to be going in the right direction, and alighted at the lower end of Queen Street as she had been instructed to. It was not difficult to find Toby's, a small shabby restaurant with glass-topped tables and a milk bar.

It was just three minutes to four. She went

15

in and sat down. At one table a woman sat feeding a small grubby-faced boy ice-cream out of a glass dish. There was no one else in the shop. A waitress came from the back to take her order. She said that she was waiting for someone and with as much nonchalance as she could assume she lit a cigarette. Every time a man appeared to pause at the door her heart lurched.

Silly! she admonished herself. New Zealand was a healthy country both physically and morally. Its crime rate was low. No one was going to do anything to her in a restaurant in a busy street — even if it were a definitely second-class restaurant and not the kind of place where a gentleman would arrange to meet a lady. But the husky voice had belonged to no gentleman, she was sure of that. Nevertheless, if she had gone down to Christchurch without finding out this mysterious information about Aunt Laura's death she would have been angry with herself for her cowardice. At any moment now her informant would arrive and she would listen to what he had to say. That was her duty to poor old Aunt Laura whom she hadn't seen since she was a child and whom she couldn't remember at all.

The child had finished his ice-cream and was scuffing his feet on the floor. His mother paid at the counter, gathered up her string shopping bag in one hand, grabbed the child with the other and went out. A siren hooted in the harbour. A tram clattered past. Two more women came in and ordered tea. Antonia stubbed out her cigarette and lit another. Her hand was trembling slightly. She could see herself in the dusty mirror on the wall opposite, fatigue smudges under her eyes, her mouth drooping. She looked small and plain. Her hat hid her silky dark red hair. No man would have looked at her twice as she was now, with her face empty of vitality, and her eyes defiantly hiding their uneasiness.

A fine foreign correspondent she would make, as nervous as this on her first hint of adventure. She began composing an article for her old paper, the *Roundabout*.

'Someone had spilt some milk on the table. I wanted to call the waitress to wipe it up, but didn't dare, as I should have to explain again that I was waiting until my mysterious friend came before I gave my order. Friend!...'

But perhaps he would be a friend. One shouldn't leap to conclusions. Punctuality, however, was not one of his virtues. It was a quarter past four and no man had set foot inside the place.

She had had time to calm down now, and even decided that she would have tea while she waited. If he hadn't come by the time she had finished her tea she would go.

The two women at the other table were talking in loud voices. The waitress came in again and Antonia beckoned to her and gave her order. When the tea came she found she could pour it without her hand shaking. Every minute that went by she grew calmer. The tea was good, too. It took away some of her fatigue. She began to see more clearly. This wasn't a nightmare where one never saw the bogey but knew he lurked always just beyond the edge of darkness. She was awake and someone had played a stupid joke on her.

But *why?*

Somewhere a clock struck the half hour. Antonia finished her tea and got up. Tomorrow in Christchurch Simon or Iris might be able to explain. She would worry no more about it now.

She paid her bill and left the shabby down-at-heel restaurant that unfortunately was her first impression of a new country and went out into the warm bright autumn afternoon. When she got back to the hotel after a leisurely loitering past shop windows it was past five o'clock. But there would still be time to snatch a nap before dinner.

She hurried up to her room and fitted the

18

key into the door.

The bed was as she had left it, rumpled from her brief rest. But she hadn't left her two suitcases open on the floor, their contents dishevelled!

In one moment it was perfectly clear to her. The appointment at the restaurant had been a ruse to get her out of the way while she was robbed. But of what? She had nothing of any great material value. The husky-voiced intruder wouldn't want nylon underclothing, or her one good evening frock. He didn't even want her wrist watch which she had left on the dressing table and that did have a certain value.

In fact, after a hasty check-up, there didn't seem to be anything missing. Nevertheless Antonia was deeply disturbed. The whole thing was odd, curiously phoney, almost as if someone were trying to frighten her. Someone ought to be told about it. She went down to the hotel office and reported the happening to the manager.

The manager was a small man with a dark edging of moustache on his upper lip and an expressionless face. He showed concern and instantly went up to Antonia's room with her.

"But you say there's nothing missing," he said, looking at the open suitcases, his thin rather feminine brows knitted in perplexity.

"Nothing that I can think of at the moment."

"You had no valuables?"

"Only my wrist watch that hadn't been taken. And some pearls. They're here, too." She produced the flat worn box. Mummy had given them to her when she was eighteen. Mummy — another life! Uncomfortably the nightmare was coming back.

"I'll get the hotel detective to look into it," the manager said. "But it's odd. You say you had this telephone call. Did you carry some information, perhaps, that his person would want?"

"I'm not a secret service agent," Antonia snapped nervily. "It was he who said he had something to tell me about an aunt of mine who died in Auckland recently."

She saw the manager didn't altogether believe her. She didn't blame him. it was an unlikely story. But it was a story that must have a conclusion.

At the request of the manager the hotel detective who had a broad stupid face and thin ferreting hands — his hands did what his eyes should have — came up in a few moments and asked her a number of questions. She told the story again.

The two men eyed the open suitcases. The detective stubbed one with a shiny patent leather toe.

"You've come a long journey, Miss Webb?"

"From England."

"Flew all the way?"

"Yes."

"It's a tiring trip. Very tiring."

Antonia looked at him levelly.

"Are you suggesting that in my fatigue I'm imagining all this?"

"Not at all, Miss Webb. Though one does begin to unpack—"

"Quite," said the manager.

"And then lie down, perhaps," said the detective.

"And dream up an appointment made over the telephone," finished Antonia.

"Well — it could be possible. And since you say there's nothing missing—"

Antonia clenched her hands. Suddenly she wanted these two stupid creatures out of her room. They might not be as stupid as they looked — and after all they didn't want trouble in the hotel. Their explanation was as reasonable as any other — for instance, that someone had followed her into the lobby when she had signed the register, noted her room number and then taken a room himself where he could come along the balcony outside. She wanted to ask that all the guests be checked. But if nothing had been stolen what charge could she make? Especially when two reasonably intelligent men thought that in the fatigue following a long plane journey she had forgotten that she had started to unpack.

"All right then," she said abruptly. "We'll drop it. I'm sorry I've bothered you."

The restaurant with the dirty glass-topped tables, the open suitcases, the two politely staring men, the thick voice over the telephone, were all part of the nightmare. She only wanted to sleep.

At eight o'clock the next morning the telephone rang again. She was disgusted that her hand trembled when she put it out to pick up the receiver.

"Hullo," she said tentatively.

"Hullo. Is that Miss Antonia Webb?" came a male voice, pleasantly slow, as utterly unlike her caller of yesterday as clear water from muddy.

"Yes, it is."

"I'm calling from Christchurch. My name's Conroy. Dougal Conroy. Your cousin may have mentioned me. I'm acting in your late aunt's estate."

"Oh, yes, Mr. Conroy. Simon did mention you." (Actually it was Iris's words she remembered – 'Dougal Conroy's a dear, but so cautious.') Cautious or not, his was the first friendly

22

voice she had heard since she had arrived. She found it enchanting.

"Simon has made the suggestion that I should meet your plane and get the brief business details over first. I gather that after that you'll be absorbed in the wedding."

"That would be wonderful, Mr. Conroy. I'm catching the plane that leaves here at midday. There's just one thing I want to do before I leave Auckland. Can you tell me where Aunt Laura is buried. I'd like to go and see her grave."

He had to go away to get that information, but presently he had it, and assuring her briskly that he would be at the airport when her plane arrived her rang off.

It was amazing how one friendly voice could cheer one up. Hurrying to finish dressing Antonia was almost prepared to believe that the hotel manager had been right last night and she was wrong. Even when she was searching in her bags for a clean blouse and found that that old letter from Aunt Laura, the one with the Peruvian stamps, had been accidentally pulled half out of the envelope and a bit ripped off she thought nothing of it. The letter was two years old, the missing bit where it had split along the crease was probably floating around somewhere among her underclothing. The thief wouldn't have found much to that.

23

But he couldn't have been a thief because nothing was missing.

The caretaker of the cemetery showed Antonia where Aunt Laura's grave was. She laid her bunch of roses on the mounded earth already beginning to flatten. Two withered wreaths still lay on the grave, the writing on the cards blurred with rain and dew.

Poor Aunt Laura, Antonia thought, travelling in every country on earth as the desire moved her for the splendid peaks of the Himalayas, or the flower-starred valleys of the Austrian Tyrol, or the golden pagodas of China, or the sun and dust and heat of Mexico. She shifted her backgrounds as other people shifted furniture in their homes, seeking change, colour, stimulation. And now she lay in this bleak shadeless grave with only two withered wreaths as a tribute to her.

Antonia stopped to read the cards. One said simply,

*For Aunt Laura. From Simon.*

And the other,

*In loving and sorrowful memory. Iris.*

Antonia walked quietly away, thinking, "I'm glad she had Iris. So far from home she had someone. Iris must be a nice person."

# II

It seemed to Dougal that he was hemmed in by women. There was his mother, there was Ethel, there was Miss Fox at the office. And now there was this strange English girl, Antonia Webb.

He hadn't been very enthusiastic about the suggestion that he should meet the girl, but the women thought another woman in his life would be just fine. There was no reason on earth why his dealings with the Mildmays should not have been confined strictly to his office. In answer to this his mother said that since they were going to be living just up the hill one ought to be neighbourly. Besides, the whole thing was so enormously fascinating.

That word was his mother's. She saw dramatic possibilities in everything, and her curiosity was unbelievable. If it had been Mrs. Lucas, then butcher (a man whose soul was wrapped up in slabs of meat), moving up to the ramshackle old house on the hilltop Henrietta would have said he was planning to keep women. Or if it were the newspaper boy she would say he was running a gambling saloon. She had the type of mind that had to embroider everything. So one could expect that with a couple like the Mildmays who did have a certain air of mystery, Henrietta's imagination would run riot.

Much as he would have liked to, Dougal knew it was no use trying to keep secret the fact that the Hilltop was taken. Henrietta spent the greater part of her day at her upstairs sitting-room window which overlooked the road running up to the Hilltop, and she saw everyone who came and went. She also noticed instantly the lights were switched on in the empty windows of the big house, and this precipitated the lengthy enquiry that Dougal had known was inevitable.

"Dougal! Ethel!" Her penetrating voice had come excitedly down the stairs. "Come quickly. I think there must be burglars at the Hilltop."

Dougal didn't shout from the bottom of the stairs because he knew it was useless. His mother was slightly deaf. He came up to the picturesque untidy room with its embarrassing collection of photographs of himself at various sizes, its comfortable chairs (his mother was a large woman and liked comfort), its book-lined walls that held every type of book from Hans Andersen to the Decameron, and its superb view of the tussocky hill that leaned its golden bosom against the apple green sunset sky.

All the long windows of the old white two-winged house on the crest of the hill were lighted.

"No, Mother," said Dougal, "what burglars would be stupid enough to put all the lights on?"

"Then who is it up there?" Henrietta demanded. "Should we notify the police?"

"The new owners would hardly appreciate that."

"Who?"

"The new owners," Dougal shouted.

Henrietta looked at him with her prominent indignant eyes. It seemed to Dougal that indignation was their most frequent expression and that he was the reason for it.

"Dougal, you didn't tell me that the Hilltop was sold."

"The sale was only finalised last week, Mother."

"Last week! Seven whole days ago. You make me live in ignorance of what is going on under my very nose."

Dougal moved his hands resignedly. It was

useless to point out to Henrietta that the first essential when one followed the profession of law was discretion. His father, in thirty years, had not been able to convince her of that, so how could he whom she had always expected to come to her with everything. His mother was an incurable gossip and like all gossips she liked to be first among her friends with new tidbits. She found it humiliating to hear from others what her own son had known, professionally, for some time.

But he admitted that he could have told her the Hilltop was sold. There would have been no harm in that.

"I'm sorry, Mother. The transaction wasn't completed until today. The Mildmays are moving in at once. Or rather Simon Mildmay's fiancée is. They're being married in a few days."

Henrietta sat down, spreading out her wide lap. Her broad, plain, highly-coloured face was full of charm and benignity.

"A wedding! How exciting! Now, Dougal, be sweet and tell me about these people."

He wasn't very good at describing people. On the other hand, if Henrietta had seen the two of them come into his office she would have known how to make him see them: the tall rather stout man with small puffy blue eyes, pink skin and plump hands, and the woman

28

who must have been in her early thirties, but who was as small and slim as a half-grown girl, with a pointed sharp-boned face and a great rope of hair the colour of champagne. It was only the faint lines at the corners of her eyes, or perhaps the eyes themselves, shrewd, intelligent, a greenish grey, that indicated her real age.

But he wasn't possessed of the ability to make Henrietta see them, nor to describe the interest they roused in him. In the first place Simon Mildmay seemed an unlikely type of man for a woman like Iris Matthews to fall in love with. His hair was thinned well back from his pink fleshy forehead, his constant smile was amiable but had a vacuity that should have been disturbing to an intelligent woman. Iris didn't look as if she lacked intelligence. But Simon adored her, his adoration was so obvious that it was almost embarrassing to an onlooker, and Dougal guessed that Iris would enjoy that. At odd moments he had caught a queer hungry look about her as if once she had been starved and was in constant fear of it happening again. That might have explained her reason for being so excited about marrying Simon, about buying that big old house that no one yet had successfully run as a guest house. They were possessions. Again, his intuition told him that

Iris would like possessions.

Neither of them had told him anything of their background. They had merely appointed him to put through the transfer of the Hilltop, and to prove the will of the old aunt, Laura Mildmay, who had died in Auckland three weeks ago. He had no personal interest in the two of them – though he had a suspicion that that would be forced on him by the mere fact that they were going to be neighbours, and that his womenfolk possessed this insatiable curiosity.

Then of course there was the question of the other beneficiary under the will, the girl still in England. He hadn't agreed that there was any necessity to send for her until he began to discover the size of the estate. Even then there was no actual need for her to make the long journey. But her coming was a family matter and not one that called for his professional advice.

Knowing of old the uselessness of trying to withhold any information from Henrietta if she really intended to have it, that first night that the windows were lighted in the Hilltop house Dougal told her the facts he knew – that Iris Matthews had been a companion and later a nurse to old Miss Mildmay and that Simon, the old lady's nephew and executor, had come out from England and fallen in love with Iris. Now that Miss Mildmay was dead they had both decided they would like to stay permanently in New Zealand, using Simon's legacy to buy the old guest house on Scarborough Hill. And lastly that they had sent for an English cousin, the other beneficiary under the will, to come for their wedding.

"How old is this girl and what does she do?" Henrietta asked.

"I understand she does journalism."

"Fine! We can talk about Fleet Street."

"You sound as if you're going to know her personally, Mother," Dougal said resignedly.

"Of course I am. One must be neighbourly. In any case, you may marry her."

"Mother! These fantastic conclusions you come to!" But he was used to it. Henrietta had had him married to every female under forty who had set foot on Scarborough Hill during the last ten years. As if three women in his life were not enough!

Henrietta didn't have a spyglass, which was her one concession to decent behaviour. But her own two eyes, mild and benevolent, could see an awful long way. The day after Simon Mildmay had taken possession of the Hilltop Henrietta reported excitedly that there were guests there already.

"How odd," she said. "Even before they're married, and they've hardly any staff either. Only that skinny little woman called Bella and her son. Anyway, I don't think it's very wise of them to be living up there together before they're married. I'm not narrow-minded, but other people are."

"Now Mother," Dougal remonstrated, "you know very well that Simon's not living up there. He's staying at an hotel down in Sumner. And who," he added, "are the guests?"

"I don't know that. I just see a light burning half the night in the wing they said they weren't using until it was renovated. Iris doesn't sleep in that wing, and neither does Bella nor her son. Ethel found that out. And if Simon isn't living there he might just as well be. They say he keeps those little parrot things, budgerigars, and that he's infatuated with them. I think they're a blind."

"A blind, Mother?"

"Yes. To make him seem more simple than he is. No normal man would be crazy about birds. He's going to be fat. I don't trust fat men. They laugh in their bellies and you never know what they're thinking."

It was true that you didn't know what Simon Mildmay was thinking, but it was probably because he wasn't thinking at all. Dougal discounted ninety per cent of his mother's sensational statements. But he was a little mystified about the light in the unused wing which he himself began to notice burnt every night.

Then there was the mild surprise of discovering the value of Laura Mildmay's New Zealand estate, and after that the letter from Antonia Webb saying that she was arriving.

But the women were nearly driving him mad.

"Now, Dougal, put that nice tie on that I gave you for Christmas. You never wear the ties I give you," Henrietta complained as he left the breakfast table that morning.

Dougal thought distastefully of the tie which was one of his mother's typical choices, too bright a blue with a design of yellow and green squiggling things that looked like fish. It was the sort of tie that a fellow like Simon Mildmay who kept birds should wear.

"I'm keeping that for special occasions," he shouted.

"This is a special occasion, dear."

And Ethel, carrying dishes from the breakfast table, turned in the doorway to give him the fat companionable giggle that came from somewhere deep down beneath her broad bosom.

"Ethel gets sillier every day," Henrietta sighed, as she went out. "If that girl would make one intelligent remark I'd sing psalms."

"Then dismiss her," said Dougal.

"Because she giggles? That would be hardly fair. And she is a wonderful cook."

Henrietta had been saying that for five years. Dougal knew that as long as Ethel wanted to stay she would stay. But he tried to imagine bringing a girl home to dinner and having Ethel give her breathy chuckle down his back with each course she served.

He went to his room and put on a sober pinspot tie he had chosen for himself. He smoothed his thick unruly fair hair and looked at his fair-skinned face in the mirror. It was tidy and unmemorable, he thought. Once a girl had told him his smile was the sweetest she had ever seen. That had embarrassed him. He had thought she was a little drunk. She had had red hair and he hadn't taken out a red-headed girl since.

He knew exactly the kind of girl he wanted to marry. She was to be small and dark-haired with a calm face and hands that she kept still. She was to be pleasant to look at and intelligent and quiet. In a word, she was to be completely opposite to the women who surrounded him: his big, happy, restless, inquisitive mother with her voice that she pitched high enough to reach her own deaf ears, giggling Ethel, sharp-faced, sharp-voiced Miss Fox at the office who seemed to him all staccato, like the sound her flying fingers made on the typewriter keys. A quiet, soft, restful woman his wife would be.

In the meantime there was the appointment to be kept at the airport, for the purpose of telling the English girl what facts he was permitted to about her inheritance.

At Harewood, while he waited on the windy airstrip for the plane to come nosing down, he had the faintest stirring of excitement. The girl's voice over the phone this morning had sounded jittery, as if she were a nervous type not fit to be travelling alone, but it had had a nice quality. Supposing by some miracle she should be quiet-faced, dark-eyed, the kind of girl who got uncomfortably into his dreams.

But, no. It was too much to hope for, he realized, when he saw the girl step out of the plane, and he knew by instinct that she was Antonia Webb.

She was carrying her hat in her hand and as she came down the steps the wind immediately caught her hair and swept it up in a shining mass. It was a subtle shade of red, dark, polished, more the colour of rosewood. But red, nevertheless. And of course she would have the kind of thin, animated, clear-skinned face that went with it, and the tall, small-waisted body. She was the kind of girl most men would admire,

Dougal realised at once. But not him. She wasn't his type. His small stirring of excitement died. He had a vague sense of disappointment. She was just another client and, he sensed, probably a troublesome one, for a girl with that kind of face wasn't going to care to be left in the dark about anything.

He went towards her, holding out a polite hand.

"Miss Webb?" he enquired.

She smiled. Her face did have animation. It lit up. Inwardly he sighed. She was going to be the awkward type, not meek, not accepting. Well, Simon Mildmay could deal with that.

"Yes. You're Mr. Conroy, aren't you. How nice of you to meet me."

"Not at all. Your cousin thought it was a good idea. We have to have a chat at some stage."

"Yes, of course." Suddenly she caught his arm. "Look, do you see that man? Oh, he's gone inside now."

"Who? Where?" Dougal looked round bewilderingly. "Is he a friend of yours?"

"Oh, no. He just sat behind me in the plane. He seemed to be watching me. You know that feeling of eyes boring into your back."

Dougal looked gloomily at her dark shining head. Some men did admire that shade of hair.

The girl looked at him with her eyes suddenly too intelligent.

"I guess that does sound fanciful. But he was watching me. When we landed at Paraparamu he followed me into the cafeteria, and sat at a table opposite. Not only that, but he seemed to be laughing at me. Inside himself. As if he knew something that I didn't and it was amusing."

"Did he speak to you?"

"No."

"Bit slow, wasn't he?" Dougal observed. "Shall we get your bags?"

The girl had flushed. Her voice became stiff.

"I'm not that kind of person, Mr. Conroy."

"What kind?" Dougal asked rather indifferently, leading the way over to the luggage trolley.

"The kind who is always expecting to be picked up," she snapped.

He looked at her in mortification.

"Oh, I'm sorry, Miss Webb. I didn't mean that at all. But that isn't to say someone might not want to — to form an acquaintance with you. Now which are your bags? I have my car here."

The girl produced her luggage check and pointed out the bags. Dougal picked them up and took her over to the car park.

"I'll drive you to Scarborough," he said. "You may like to have tea or something on the way."

"No, thank you," she answered. She was still offended with him. Her dark blue eyes were gleaming.

Dougal opened the car door for her, then got in himself and started the engine.

"What was this fellow like?" he asked seriously, trying to make amends.

"Oh – dark hair and eyes, very pale skin. His nose was thin and slightly crooked. Look, Mr. Conroy," she said suddenly, "I'd have taken no notice of all this if something odd hadn't happened to me in Auckland yesterday. I had a telephone call to meet someone in a café and while I was out my bags were searched."

Slightly startled, Dougal looked at her.

"Are you joking?"

"Indeed I'm not." Her voice was vehement. "They tried to tell me in the hotel that I'd imagined it – that I'd started unpacking and forgotten – but I'm not that irresponsible."

"Who was the person you were to meet?"

"I haven't the faintest idea. All he said was that he knew something about Aunt Laura's death. But he didn't turn up, so I guess it was just a ruse. But why?"

"I can't imagine. Sounds odd to me. Did

you miss anything?"

The girl looked at him with her bright alert eyes. He realised suddenly and a little uncomfortably that she was reading his thoughts, that she knew he was thinking she was a little overawed by her long trip, a little fanciful and neurotic. He didn't think that altogether. But the story was queer — the sort of thing that might happen in Marseilles or Chicago, the sort of thing an imaginative girl travelling for the first time might dream up. They said she'd been on the stage a bit. That was how she looked, too, dramatic, highly sensitive.

"I didn't miss anything," she said in a quiet closed voice. And he knew, a little regretfully, that she had given him up as a confidant. Temporarily, anyway. If anything further happened and he saw it with his own eyes he would be right on her side.

"Well, let's not worry about it," he said. "There was nothing unusual about your aunt's death. I have the death certificate, so whoever it was was bluffing. I hope you'll like New Zealand, Miss Webb. Your cousin has a nice place. It's a bit windy and isolated, it wouldn't appeal to everyone. But Miss Matthews seems an energetic person. I should think anything she started she would make a success of."

"You mean Iris? What's she like?" The girl's

voice was still withdrawn, but it couldn't quite restrain its curiosity. Well, why shouldn't she be interested in her new relative? That didn't mean she was the inquisitive type.

"She's a very nice person," Dougal answered quite uninformatively. "Your cousin seems very much in love. How long do you plan to stay in New Zealand, Miss Webb?"

"Oh, call me Antonia," the girl said, a little impatiently, as if formality irritated her. "I don't really know. It depends. Tell me about this legacy. No one's told me a word yet. I expect it isn't much. Poor old Aunt Laura. I can't remember her, you know, so it was awfully sweet of her to remember me."

"As I said, that was really my object in meeting you," Dougal explained. "They thought it was a good opportunity for me to tell you what I am able to."

"What you're able to? What do you mean?"

"Well, there's rather an odd clause in your aunt's will that you don't inherit any capital until you're twenty-four, and that until then you shouldn't be told the extent of your inheritance."

"I wonder why," said Antonia.

"That we don't know. But I imagine it's meant to protect you from fortune hunters."

"How humorous! I couldn't be getting that much money."

40

"No, to be quite candid I don't think you are. I haven't got the estimate of your aunt's English estate, but after Simon's legacy of ten thousand is paid there won't be a great surplus from the New Zealand one. If your aunt has been away from England for some years I shouldn't think she would have left a great deal of capital there. But I'm making enquiries."

"I say!" Antonia exclaimed. "Does old Simon get ten thousand? Golly! That's quite something, isn't it?"

"It's not to be sneezed at," Dougal commented briefly. If Miss Mildmay's English estate did prove to be negligible it hardly seemed fair that Simon should get twice as much as this girl would. But that was for her to dispute if she wished, and she couldn't do so until she was cognisant of all the facts.

"Your cousin said you were twenty-three, Miss – Antonia. Is that right?"

"Quite right. But I'll be twenty-four in six weeks, and I'm not likely to be pursued by fortune hunters in the interval. I suppose Aunt Laura thought that by twenty-four I'd have enough sense to avoid them. But she's suffering from an hallucination about her money, isn't she?"

"Probably at the time the will was made ten years ago she wasn't. I should think in the interval she's lived on her capital. What do you know about her personally?"

"Well, I know she's been a widow for as long as I can remember and I think she was left comfortably off. She must have been because she's lived in just about every country there is since then. But I should imagine she'd just about used up her cash doing so. Is there really ten thousand left for Simon?"

Dougal reflected. Then he said, "There can be no harm in telling you that her New Zealand estate is being proved at sixteen thousand pounds. Death duties will be fairly considerable, but the balance will be yours – when you've had that birthday."

Antonia smiled, as if birthdays were pleasant to her. Her face had a look of young excitement.

"I say, Mr. Conroy, this is awfully thrilling. It's happened so suddenly, me being here, being rich – "

"Probably about four thousand pounds," Dougal reminded her.

"That's riches to me. If you'd tried to live on newspaper articles and bit parts on the stage – It's this clear blue sky in New Zealand that's so entrancing, Mr. Conroy."

"If I have to call you Antonia I can't imagine why you don't bother to find out what my name is."

Her eyes on him were no longer troubled, but laughing and happy. She was as changeable as the sea spreading itself away limitlessly beneath the high dangerous Scarborough cliffs.

"Tell me," she said in her warm voice.

Suddenly he was remembering the red-headed girl who had made him feel an ass about his smile.

"Dougal," he said gloomily.

When he got back to his office after leaving Antonia at the Hilltop the mail was on his table. He picked up the top letter and read it. He drew in his breath on a long note of surprise. He read the letter again and pressed the buzzer on his desk.

In a moment the door opened and Miss Fox stood there, her thin bluish nose quivering, her eyes gleaming behind their black-rimmed glasses.

"I say, Miss Fox, did you see this?" It was unnecessary to ask that question. Apart from opening all his mail as one of her secretarial duties the gleam in her eye showed that Miss Fox was as interested as he.

"The English letter, Mr. Conroy? Yes, I did. That old woman must have been something of a dark horse."

"I'll say she must have. We've really stumbled

43

on something. Telephone and see if you can arrange for Simon Mildmay to come in first thing tomorrow morning."

He wasn't thinking of the work or the profit involved in winding up an estate. He was thinking of Antonia Webb's excited eyes as she said, "Four thousand pounds! That's riches to me." Four thousand! The thing was humorous.

And at the same time a curious little picture came into his mind. It was like delayed vision, something he had seen a short time ago and not consciously noted, the tall man in a raincoat getting casually out of a taxi half way up the Scarborough hill, as if he were meaning to get the fresh air that blew over the crest of the hill from the sea far below. It was like a tiny picture in a bubble, the man paying the taxi driver and all the time looking up the hill, the way Dougal had just driven Antonia.

Probably it was merely coincidental that someone should be wanting a tramp on the hillside, probably it was nothing whatever to do with the man Antonia had complained of in the plane. Whoever would want to shadow her? It was unreasonable.

But it was odd that he should remember that, and that the significance of it should come to him just as he was reading this letter. Very odd, and a little disturbing.

# III

In the big airy hall the first thing Antonia saw was the large bird cage with its darting twittering occupants. There were flashes of green, of yellow, of the most delicate blue. The birds hung by their minute beaks to the netting, they ran up and down miniature ladders, rang tiny tinkly bells placed there for their amusement, and perched in couples on twigs to make love, kissing one another about their feathery throats with ineffable tenderness, and making the most fond whispering sounds. They made a blur of moving colour in the otherwise colourless hall with its white plaster walls and long uncurtained windows.

Dougal Conroy had not come in with her. He said he would not intrude on her meeting with her relatives. He had put her bags inside the door and had gone, leaving her feeling a little lost and lonely.

The rambling old house on the summit of the hill had been rather a surprise to her. It no doubt had an odd sort of attraction for anyone who liked isolation, perched up there, its tall windows vulnerable both to the sea wind and to the gusty one that came down the long shining curve of the sky from the mountain range a hundred miles across the plains in the west. Its untended garden had possibilities. Rock terraces could be built to cut off the wind, the little stunted rhododendrons and hydrangeas could be pruned and nourished, the great sprawling flaxbush whose leaves made a constant clashing like swords could be removed from the centre of the lawn where it was unwieldy and untidy, the half-grown pines along the east wall could be trimmed so that they would grow thickly enough to provide a shelter from the sea wind. In the process of her walk up the gravelled drive Antonia could visualise all that, as no doubt Iris and Simon had done before her. She could see striped garden chairs where there was an old disused sandpit in the most sheltered corner, and a flagstone terrace in the L shape of the house, with tubs of geraniums and little spiky trees set along the edge.

She could understand Iris's and Simon's enthusiasm about the possibilities of the place.

But she wondered if they had her queer sense of desolation and loneliness as the wind stirred round the house and the sound of the sea, like recurring thunder, came from the rocks far below. Sunshine lay like a carpet over the golden hillside, the wind-smoothed tussocks shone like the backs of sleeky groomed animals. But there was that constant sense of desolation that she couldn't shake off when she stood in the light airy hall.

Then Simon came clattering down the stairs. His face, much bigger and broader and friendlier than she remembered it, and his outstretched hand, did something to reassure her.

"It's grand to see you, Tonia," he declared, pressing a soft moist kiss on her cheek. (Were those the kind of kisses he gave Iris?) "Conroy said he'd meet you — get the business side over quickly. Ten thousand pounds, eh? And God knows how much for you. Poor old Aunt Laura. She was a champion. Iris and I thought it would be nice if we could all share this together. That's why we sent for you. Even if you don't decide to stay it was a trip, wasn't it? We were disappointed when you had to put it off for a fortnight. Hope you're all right now."

"Simon, used you always talk this much?" Antonia asked, laughing. She remembered him as a silent person, affable and good-tempered

47

but with not a word to say. Now he was positively hearty.

He laughed, too, his pale blue eyes disappearing in soft pink curves of flesh. "No. I didn't. But this is all so staggering. A turn of the old luck. And Iris! But wait till you see her. Do you know, her hair's so long she can sit on it. Masses of it." He curved his hands, his lips pursed sensually as if he were feeling the hair in them. Iris must sometimes let it down and let him touch it, and now he was remembering the warm alive feel of it.

Then he jerked his head up as if he were arousing himself.

"We're upstairs fixing the carpet in your room. It only arrived this morning. We thought we wouldn't get it ready in time. Come and meet Iris. Don't you like my little birds? They're the most fascinating creatures, especially this little yellow fellow. He's beginning to talk."

He bent a moment over the cage, watching absorbedly the bright quick movement within. He had on a pair of baggy grey flannel trousers and a very old loose striped sweater. His body within it was rotund and too fat. His skin was pink and soft, his full lips a little loose, his eyes perhaps because of shyness not quite direct. His enthusiasm, Antonia remembered, had always been for little things, guinea pigs, tadpoles, moths and beetles. But now there was a woman. Who was this woman who wanted to marry nice kind old Simon?

Even as she wondered there were light quick steps on the stairs and Antonia looked up to see the girl coming down. Surely she was only sixteen, this small light creature in a blue artist's smock, with a smudge of dust on her forehead and her fair almost colourless hair twisted in a rope round her head. As Simon had said, it was her hair that caught one's eye. it was so luxuriant, and it had that pale shine, like light on silvery pussy willow buds.

"Antonia!" she cried in a high voice. "How wonderful that you've got here at last. I hope you didn't mind Dougal Conroy going to meet you. He's rather sweet, isn't he? Simon and I did want to get your room finished before you arrived. It's just done now. If you had come when you were first supposed to you would have found us in complete chaos. We're still all at sixes and sevens, as you can see. Aren't Simon's birds sweet? He's crazy about them. But do come upstairs."

"You might give me a chance to introduce Antonia to you," Simon put in in his slow serious voice.

Iris laughed. Her teeth were little and very close together. Her green eyes rayed fine lines at the corners. She wasn't a sixteen-year-old girl after all. And if you took away her hair with its silvery shine, like the down on a pussy willow catkins, her face would be almost plain.

"Now, don't be so formal, Simon. As if we don't know each other." Iris leaned from the bottom step of the stairs to kiss Antonia. Only that way was she on a level with Antonia. "Simon, isn't she pretty?"

"I might repeat that about you," said Antonia, speaking for the first time. The clear pallor of Iris's cheeks, her green eyes and pale hair fitted almost uncomfortably into this cool white house, like an underwater nymph, or a ghost. Almost shivery. And there was old Simon nodding slowly, as pleased and proud as a king with a new fabulous empire.

Iris had begun to move quickly up the stairs. She gave the impression of never being still.

"Come on, Antonia. Come and see your room. We've put some pains into it because if you stay it must be nice. And if you don't it will be our private guest room. This place wants an awful lot doing to it, but of course we're concentrating on our own living quarters first. We're keeping the upstairs part of this wing entirely for ourselves."

"We don't plan to open until the spring," Simon said behind Antonia.

"No," said Iris. "No one would want to come up here in the winter. It's entirely a summer place. Simon and I thought it would be wonderful to have three months to ourselves and just get the renovations done at our convenience. We've all sorts of plans. I want to make this place like one of those delightful little places on the Riviera. Bright blue shutters, flower baskets, things like that. We got it dirt cheap, of course."

"With Aunt Laura's money," Simon put in.

"Only part of it, darling," Iris said a little sharply. "Look, Antonia, this is your room."

She led the way into a large room charmingly furnished in deep yellow and apple green. The windows faced down the hillside over the rooftops of Sumner and the gentle curving bay.

"Simon told me you had red hair," Iris said. "That's why I chose these colours. But I love yellow, anyway."

Antonia was moved by the thoughtfulness Iris had shown.

"The room's lovely," she said warmly. "How very kind you are."

"Not a bit. We're so glad to have you. Me especially. It's been lonely here at nights when Simon goes down to his hotel. Just Bella and Gussie and me, and Bella and Gussie are downstairs. Now we'll leave you to change. Dinner's at seven. There'll only be the three of us, and Bella isn't an awfully good cook yet, but she's learning. Come along, Simon. Let Antonia change."

"But I'm only going down to that hotel for two more nights," Simon said in a loud triumphant voice. "Aren't I, love?"

He bent and kissed Iris on the back of her neck. Antonia thought of how his lips would be moist against her skin. Iris's little white face remained quite calm.

"Yes, darling. So you are."

It seemed to Antonia that she might have been speaking to a child.

Dinner was in the big dining-room that was as yet so sparsely furnished that sounds echoed. The long windows looked towards the sea that in the growing darkness seemed an immense distance down, as if they were perched on top of the world. There was always the sound of its slow drag and crash on the rocks. The wind, sighing over the tussocky hillside and rattling the windows, never ceased.

The room was draughty and chilly with a feel of early frost. Iris, who had changed into a low-necked dinner dress that showed her white shoulders and outlined her small breasts, looked as if she would never be still long enough to feel cold. She was talking incessantly about her plans for the hotel.

"Don't you see the possibilities these big rooms have? All that old plaster moulding will be pulled down, we'll have the walls painted, a new fireplace put in, window seats round these lovely windows. And I'm really going to let myself go on the furnishings. I've a colour scheme planned. The bedrooms won't be numbered, they'll go by colours, the blue, the gold, the green and so on. And of course there's oceans of plumbing to do, hot and cold water to be put in all the bedrooms and a couple more bathrooms. And then there's the bar. I've offered to let Simon design that, but he hasn't had any brilliant ideas yet. Have you, darling?"

Simon, his mouth full, waved his fork in a large gesture.

"The place is yours, love, bar and all. I'll just mix the drinks."

He gave his loud delighted childish laugh. Antonia glanced at Iris. She was frowning slightly.

"I doubt if I could even trust you to do that." The next moment the sharpness (had it been sharpness?) was out of her voice and she was saying with amused tolerance, "Simon's so helpless! Has he always been like that, Antonia?"

Antonia looked at Simon's amiable face.

"Am I in a position to judge, Simon? We haven't seen a lot of each other. I used to think he was a horrid small boy."

"I'm quite sure he was," said Iris.

Simon gave his wide smile and turned his attention with renewed interest to his plate.

The meal was served by a thin-faced woman with a stooped back and an air of overwhelming tiredness. Iris explained that that was Bella Smale whose husband was in hospital dying of tuberculosis. Her son Gussie, a sharp little scamp, untruthful and untrustworthy, lived with her. He pretended to be dumb when he got into any trouble, but he was as intelligent as the next one. He would be useful about the place if he could be trained, which sometimes seemed doubtful. Of course later there would be a complete staff.

"Well, let's show Antonia over," Simon said.

But Antonia felt enough had been said in the meantime about the hotel. She wanted to talk about the wedding, about Aunt Laura's death, and particularly about those disturbing events that had happened in Auckland.

However, neither Iris nor Simon was going to be talkative about Aunt Laura. Iris, who had been her companion for six months before she died, seemed genuinely upset, and Simon also was subdued. He had come out from England a few weeks before Aunt Laura's death because she was worried about her affairs, and as her executor and a relative she wanted him with her. Iris had met her on a passenger ship coming out to New Zealand from England, and, at the old lady's request, had become her companion.

"She was so sweet to me," she said. "The poor darling was ill then, but I didn't know that. I'm only glad I was able to help her for that short time."

"Iris saw to everything," said Simon. "She was wonderful."

"No, I wasn't. After all I owed Miss Mildmay something. I needed a job and she gave me a home as well. And then" — her voice was suddenly almost flippant — "she provided for Simon, too."

"Did she know you were going to be married?" Antonia asked.

"We don't quite know. We told her, but she was only semi-conscious for some time before she died. Now and again she'd brighten. It was a stroke, you know. She had two slight ones, and then this last one."

"Poor old Aunt Laura," said Simon. "I always remember once when I was a kid my dog got run over and killed. It broke my heart, especially when they said I couldn't have another. But one arrived a week later, a puppy in a basket with a blue ribbon round his neck. A golden cocker. He was from Aunt Laura. She knew my mother would never turn away such a cute little beggar, blue ribbon and all. She was right. I was allowed to keep him. I never forgot that."

"Simon's *enormously* sentimental," Iris sighed. "It's not always practical in this hard old life."

Antonia was pursuing her own thoughts. "What could that man have wanted to tell me about Aunt Laura's death? It must have been a hoax."

"What man?"

When Iris's attention was aroused her eyes glittered, Antonia noticed.

"Oh, I had a peculiar phone call." Antonia began to relate the incident again, but now without a great deal of conviction. Everyone had cried her down so much that she was almost beginning to wonder herself if the thing had really happened.

"I might have had a blank about the unpacking," she finished, "but there was still the phone call. No one's been able to explain that away."

Simon's mouth hung open a little. His eyes were fixed on Antonia, then as she looked at him they slid away in their customary evasive manner. Iris was saying a little breathlessly:

"How very odd! How disturbing for you! But surely it can't have meant anything." Her face seemed very thin and sharp. It almost seemed as if she were reassuring herself. Then she said slowly, "Are you quite sure—"

"That it really happened," Antonia finished. "Now please don't you start on that angle. I may be a little absent-minded, but surely not that much."

"Absent-minded," Iris repeated reflectively. "I wonder— But, you poor darling, it was upsetting for you. Nothing like that will happen to you here, I can assure you."

So she, too, was subscribing to the theory of hallucinations, Antonia thought wearily. Well, maybe everybody was right. Even Simon, with his indirect eyes. But he, suddenly, was looking a little frightened of her.

As soon as dinner was over they showed her all the rooms in the right wing of the house. The left wing, Iris said, was shut up until the workmen arrived. It wasn't fit for inspection. She began to talk happily of her plans again, and the thought came into Antonia's mind that she was marrying, not Simon, but her pet dream, a small exclusive hotel on Continental lines. It was the logical explanation. In a way it was Aunt Laura's legacy to her, and doubtless she deserved it.

At ten o'clock Simon left to go down the road to his hotel. Antonia was in her room, and through her open window the murmur of his and Iris's voice came up from the front door. Antonia sat down before her dressing table with its pretty golden drapings. She yawned and picked up her hair-brush. She was very tired. The day was a confusion of half-formed impressions. She hoped Iris was bidding Simon a genuinely affectionate goodnight. Poor old Simon, he was so naïve, so proud of Iris. After all, often one partner to a marriage loved a little more than the other. That didn't necessarily make the marriage a failure.

Antonia's thought broke off as Simon's voice, suddenly loud and a little bewildered, came up to her.

"But you'll have to tell her now that they haven't come."

Iris's reply was inaudible. Again came Simon's voice, definite in spite of its bewilderment. "They may not even come tomorrow."

"Of course they will. They've promised. Anyway, I'll see to that. For goodness' sake, don't be a fool at this stage." Iris's voice, sharply raised, was clear this time. It was Simon's that was lowered now. He said something anxiously and Iris answered, "I'll make all possible enquiries. But it *can't* be anything. It just isn't possible."

Simon made a muttered answer. Then he went tramping down the gravelled drive, and there was the sound of the front door shutting.

What was it that Simon thought she should be told? It could be nothing connected with her legacy because Dougal Conroy was looking after that. Antonia was sure that self-possessed young man would do nothing indiscreet. She had found his correctness and his discretion provocative as well as a little irritating as they had driven to the Hilltop that afternoon, but now, with the wind rising and that dreary flax-bush on the lawn giving its staccato crackles, it was comforting to think that the lights of the Conroy house were visible from here. Dougal had told her that merely as a passing remark, but now, remembering, she went to the window to lean out and stare down the darkening hillside.

"What are you doing?" came Iris's voice sharply behind her.

Antonia started so that she almost lost her balance.

"Just looking at the lights," she said. "Mr. Conroy said I'd be able to see their house from here."

"Oh, Dougal!" It seemed that Iris relaxed.

Could she have thought that Antonia was deliberately trying to eavesdrop? "Yes, that's their house — the first at the turn of the road. Dougal has a terrible mother, poor boy."

"Terrible? How?"

"Oh, she shouts the most appalling gossip at you. All exaggerated, of course. She's always looking for sensations." Iris was chatting in a friendly way now. "Can I come in and have a cigarette? It's been so lonely up here when Simon's gone at nights. But as he says it's only for two more nights. Do you hear that whistling noise?"

Antonia had already noticed the thin eerie sound that came at intervals of ten seconds or so and that seemed to grow louder as the wind rose. She had thought at first that it was fancy, or an echo in her ears.

"It's the whistling buoy," Iris said. "There are bad rocks down there. You only hear it when the wind is from the east, thank goodness. It gives me the jitters."

"Didn't you hear it before you bought this place?"

"Oh, yes. But I wouldn't let a little thing like that put me off. It's only at night when I'm alone that I think of it."

She sat down on the ottoman at the foot of the bed, and her eyes had a narrow sharp look.

Suddenly there was no softness in her face. It was all introspection. She's remembering something in her past, perhaps in her childhood, Antonia thought. Something hard and unhappy. She looks like a woman who has ghosts walking — at night, when she's alone and there are lonely sounds. Poor Simon, she was going to be too complex for him.

"Tell me what you're wearing for your wedding," Antonia invited.

Iris looked up. The tension left her face. It became animated.

"A green faille suit. Simon likes me in green. We thought it was too soon after Miss Mildmay's death for it to be anything but a quiet wedding. I haven't a hat yet. Would you like to come shopping with me tomorrow?"

"Yes, very much."

"That's nice. By the way, that telephone conversation you say you had in Auckland. Can you think of anyone who would do that to you — play a joke, for instance?"

"It would be a poor sort of joke to play on anyone. How should I know who would do it? I don't know a soul in Auckland."

"Extraordinary!" Iris murmured. "Tell me how the voice sounded."

As well as she could Antonia imitated the thick slow sound. In her own voice it sounded merely feeble and silly.

Iris laughed.

"That sounds like the villain out of the melodrama. Someone *is* having a joke on you, that is if you didn't dream the whole thing."

But her laughter had an uneasy note in it. She was by no means reassured that Antonia had dreamed the episode, and if she hadn't dreamed it then there was someone in Auckland who puzzled and disturbed her. Had she a guilty conscience? But how could she have? Aunt Laura had died of a stroke, as the medical certificate stated. Iris had nursed her faithfully for six months and now, in marrying Simon and acquiring this draughty guest house, she was getting her just reward.

Iris seemed to be following Antonia's trend of thought.

"Did Dougal Conroy tell you about your legacy?" she asked.

"He said I was getting about four thousand pounds. That seems an enormous sum to me."

Iris's lashes lowered. Her mouth had an almost prim line.

"My dear, you never know your luck. It may be much more than that."

# IV

Antonia found she couldn't sleep in her big airy bedroom. There were too many unfamiliar sounds, the washing of the sea far below, the wind breathing in heavy uneven breaths in the pine trees and rattling the sword leaves of the flaxbush, the faint melancholy whistle of the buoy, the sudden rattling of a window, ill-fitting with age. In a night or two she would be acclimatized. She would revel in the fresh cool salty air and the view down the hill to the lights of Sumner, glittering in clusters up the dark cliffs and strung in a bright semi-circle round the bay. Her ears would grow so accustomed to the constant undercurrent of sound that finally she wouldn't hear it, but would only think how quiet it was, how peaceful. On a clear night, Simon had said, you could see right across to the snow-capped mountains, like a line of foam, on the far horizon.

Simon had a childish pride in this, his first property. So had Iris, but her pride was far from childish. It was greater than Simon's, and much more complex, Antonia sensed. There was something about Iris that was hard to understand, a streak of hardness or defiance or triumph, or perhaps just plain possessiveness. She wasn't a comfortable person. But like a potent wine she had gone to Simon's head. Antonia hoped sincerely that the marriage would work out.

She began to wonder, drowsily, what kind of a hat Iris would buy in the morning. Then suddenly she was remembering the long yellowish face of the man in the plane who had kept giving her those surreptitious faintly amused glances. His interest had not been merely physical, she had been sure of that. Another thing that she was sure of was that she would see him again, but how or where her intuition could not tell her.

The wind was rising. It rattled sharply against a window that must have been left unfastened. Antonia heard the sharp chatter of it in the frame. Then there was a high note like someone calling. *O-ooo*, it went. Antonia tucked herself deeper under the blankets. One would get used to these sounds in time, but she didn't think she would stay long enough to get too acclimatized. She would have to wait until her twenty-fourth birthday, then, if her legacy were available, she would have a look at the rest of New Zealand, do some articles, and after that go home, perhaps via America. Already Aunt Laura was giving her her own footlooseness. Poor dead Aunt Laura with the withered flowers on her grave and her restless feet still.... 

That *was* someone calling. Antonia sat up abruptly. That high screech was no wind. There it was again, thin and prolonged, and at the same time the window rattled violently.

Antonia got out of bed and pulled on a wrap. She was shivering. The curtains were billowing out, filling the room with the sea smell. It wasn't her window that was rattling for, she discovered, it was firm in its frame.

She went into the passage and along to Iris's room. Iris's door was shut. Antonia tapped gently, calling at the same time:

"Iris! Iris, are you awake?"

There were quick movements within as if Iris had leapt out of bed. Then Iris was at the door, her long pale hair hanging loose over her shoulders. Simon would like to see it like that, Antonia thought. It was like a rich stream of honey, shining and luxuriant. Simon would like to bury his big hands in it, taking sensuous handfuls of it.

"What's the matter?" Iris demanded.

"That noise," said Antonia, shivering. "What is it?"

"What noise?"

"Someone calling. And a window rattling."

Iris put her hand on Antonia's arm.

"My dear girl, you're jittery. It's only the wind. The windows in this house are abominably loose. The first night I was frightened out of my wits. But you get used to it."

"It wasn't just the window rattling," Antonia said stubbornly. "It was the voice."

"The voice? Like a baby?"

"Yes, a little."

Iris laughed.

"Seagulls, darling. They used to have me fooled, too. And there's that wretched whistling buoy. I know it's disturbing. I remember now that the dining-room window was left open. It will be the one that's rattling. I'll go down and close it. Go in my room and have a cigarette."

Antonia drew the wrap closely about her. She was still shivering. "No, thank you. If you're sure that's all it is I'll go back to bed."

Iris looked at her with concern.

"Take an aspirin if you can't sleep. And if you hear that noise again it's only gulls. Extraordinary creatures. They never seem to sleep."

Antonia did take an aspirin and surprisingly enough she did sleep for a little. But later she awakened with a start and she knew with certainty that something had awakened her. The gulls again, she thought wearily. Perhaps if she closed her window she wouldn't hear them. She got out of bed, feeling cold and clammy, her heart still thumping. At the open window she leaned out to listen, and it was then that she saw the light in the opposite wing, the reputedly empty wing. Although the blind was drawn one of the long windows had lights burning behind it.

It was from that room that the sounds were coming. With a chilly sense of fear Antonia knew that. She also knew that this was something that should be investigated. If someone was crying behind a window they should be helped. Seagulls, Iris had said. But Iris must have known better than that. Then what was she up to?

Antonia's teeth were chattering audibly. She found herself longing suddenly for the sound of Dougal Conroy's cool sane voice. His house was only half a mile down the hill. But he wouldn't want to come up because someone cried in the night. It was probably Bella grieving for her sick husband. But Bella slept next to the kitchen on the ground floor. Antonia had seen her room. And a woman didn't usually cry with that abandon. Then who— Even as Antonia wondered the sound came again, thin and forlorn, so forlorn that something had to be done quickly no matter how scared she was.

This time Antonia didn't go to Iris's room. She put on slippers and her wrap and crept along the passage and down the stairs. The wind disguised the creakings her footsteps made. She was glad of her foresight in never travelling without a flashlight. Now it guided her across the big cold hall to the door that led to the other wing, the door through which Iris had refused to take her earlier that evening, saying she must wait until the plumbing and the painting had been done.

There was a key in the door. It had been turned in the lock but not taken away. Antonia turned it again gently, and as the door opened she found another stairway, dusty and narrower than the main one. She went up it quickly, not bothering too much now about the sound of her footsteps, and found herself on an uncarpeted landing. A passage ran to the left. There were doors on either side. Under one of them a thin streak of light showed.

Antonia advanced with as much boldness as she could muster and tapped on the door.

There was a faint scuffle within, then silence.

"Who's in there?" Antonia called. Her voice was loud enough, even if it were not quite steady.

No answer came.

She tapped again.

"I heard you crying and I've come to help you. Please open the door."

Again there was silence, curiously blank and guilty.

Antonia was quite sure there was someone in there. Her hand went to the door handle.

"May I come in?" she called more loudly. When still there was no answer she turned the door handle. The door was locked.

She rapped again.

"Listen," she called, "I've come to help you."

In the silence that followed she thought she could hear husky breathing within. She put her ear against the panel. Then overcome by the sense of urgency which the locked door imparted to her she slipped to her knees and put her eye to the keyhole. Almost simultaneously there was a faint click and the light went out.

As she knelt rigidly she was positive she could hear breathing, close....

# V

Half a mile down the hill Henrietta opened her door and called in her rich warm voice:

"Dougal! The light's gone out only this minute."

Dougal, awakened, stirred irritably. He knew he would have to answer his mother, otherwise her voice would be raised louder and louder until finally the people at the Hilltop heard it.

"What light?" he asked thickly.

"The one in the empty wing. The one I told you about. Just this minute it's gone out. And it's after three o'clock."

"Then why aren't you in bed?"

"I've been reading, dear. The new thriller I got from the library. The victim was strangled first and then drowned, just to make sure. I do hope there's nothing queer going on at the Hilltop with that poor little girl just arrived."

"Don't be such a liar, Mother. You're praying that something queer is going on. And," he added, now thoroughly awake, and with the problem of Antonia Webb back on his mind, "she's not little and she's by no means poor."

He must see Simon Mildmay first thing in the morning. What did it matter if they did burn a light in the empty wing until late at night? It was no one else's business.

"It's probably plumbers, Mother," he went on.

"What's that, darling?"

"Plumbers. In the empty wing."

"My dear boy, what plumber *ever* works at night? Never mind, Antonia will tell us. We'll have her to dinner after the wedding on Thursday. She'll be left alone then, I expect, that's if the other two are planning a honeymoon. You must begin to see something of her."

"Why on earth must I?"

Dougal's mother appeared at the door then, filling it with her generous bulk, his father's old shabby dressing gown that she always wore about the house at night making her seem even larger.

"Because you must marry one day, darling, and who knows, she may be just the right person."

Dougal was going to make his habitual impatient rejoinder. But suddenly he couldn't. His mother standing there in that old dressing gown, beloved because of its association, was suddenly too pathetic, too vulnerable. Some day a woman might cling to an old garment of his because it was all she had left of him. That was a thought to touch one uncomfortably. One couldn't dismiss it or laugh at it.

# VI

Before breakfast the next morning Antonia went into the garden. A light mist was clearing, leaving patches of intensely blue sky. The sea sparkled, the hillsides were patterned with sun and shadow. There was nothing desolate about the Hilltop this morning. The light wind was no more than a passing caress over the sleek tussocks, the sweep of the white gulls was full of life and joy.

But it hadn't been the gulls crying in the night, Antonia could swear. No matter how much unreality the night's events now had that was one thing of which she was certain. She looked up at the house, seeing the blank empty windows with drawn blinds in the unused wing. The window which had shown a light had been the one third from the end. If anyone were in there the blind would have been pulled by

73

now. Unless the occupant were a late sleeper.

The sound of a lawn mower came to her ears. She went round the side of the house and saw a very thin-bodied boy in a faded blue shirt and khaki shorts slowly pushing a lawn mower. His bare feet, following the cut swathe, made imprints in the wet grass. When he saw Antonia he stopped work and stared. His shaggy dark hair badly needed cutting, his small pale eyes had a sly look. Antonia realised at once who he would be, the son of Bella and her sick husband, Gussie Smale. Simon had said he wasn't very bright, but Iris had declared he had all his wits. Iris didn't like him very much, obviously. Antonia observed his ill-kempt urchin appearance. It was clear that he was lazy because of his readiness to stop work when she approached, he was probably impudent and the looseness of his smile was not very attractive, nor the sly look in his eyes. But he was only a child, not more than eleven or twelve, she guessed. Probably the kid had never had a chance.

"You're Gussie, aren't you?" she said in a friendly voice.

The boy nodded his shaggy head.

"Do you like living up here?"

"So long as I can go down to fish it's all right."

"The wind doesn't keep you awake, or — or gulls crying?"

74

"No, Miss. That doesn't. But she do sometimes."

"She?" queried Antonia softly.

He nodded vigorously.

"She were naughty last night—"

*"Gussie!"* The boy started violently at the sound of Iris's voice from an open window upstairs. The colour came darkly behind his freckled skin.

Antonia had started almost as sharply herself. Iris's voice had been like a knife. She looked up to see Iris leaning out of the window, her hair silvery in the early light. From that height her face was all angles. Like a little silver witch, Antonia thought, the unreality coming back.

"Good morning, Antonia," she called. She was smiling now. "I must tell you that Gussie is incorrigibly lazy. If you encourage him he'll stand and talk for hours. Gussie, that lawn has to be finished before you have breakfast. Now you go right ahead."

Gussie's lashes were dropped over his pale eyes. His face had a closed sulky look. He began to mutter to himself as he pushed the lawn mower.

"That's better," said Iris. "Breakfast's ready, Antonia. Bella's just called."

Antonia went slowly into the house, reflecting that Gussie didn't like Iris. Of course he was lazy and wouldn't like anyone who prodded him to work. But there was spite in his dislike for Iris. She could see that.

Who had he meant had been naughty last night?

When she went into the hall Iris was standing staring at the birds flitting and chattering in their cage. She seemed lost in thought.

"They're pretty, aren't they?" said Antonia.

Iris looked up.

"Yes, their colours are wonderful. That pale blue is a very subtle shade. Simon says he's always wanted to keep love-birds. Did you know that?" Iris's face wore an expression of tolerance, but under it Antonia could sense her impatience for Simon's childish hobby. Then she gave her brilliant smile. "But let's come and eat. Simon will be here presently and we want to get into town early, don't we? Isn't it a lovely morning. I hope it's like this tomorrow. Not that it matters much, there aren't going to be many people there."

"But it's your wedding day."

"Yes," said Iris. Her voice was low. It had a note not so much of unbelief as triumph — as if this represented a great victory for her. Who was she? Antonia wondered. What had she been before she had met Aunt Laura on a ship?

More important, what was she going to do to Simon? But Simon had his own private enthusiasms, he was not over-bright and he was infatuated with Iris. Perhaps she would make him very happy.

"I hope," said Iris as they sat down, "that you finally got to sleep last night. It was a particularly bad night for your first one here, but it's surprising how one gets used to it."

She began pouring tea. Antonia, watching her thin nervously quick hands, said, "Who sleeps in the other wing?"

Iris looked up quickly.

"No one. I told you. It's shut up."

"Then why was there a light in one of the windows?"

"A light! Surely there wasn't. When did you see it?"

"About three o'clock this morning. In fact," Antonia went on deliberately, "I heard someone crying and went along to investigate."

Iris's brows were raised in interest and astonishment.

"Darling! How brave of you! But of course there was no one. Was there?"

"No one who would open the door."

Iris leaned back in her chair.

"I told you it was the gulls. You wouldn't believe me."

"Seagulls don't switch on lights. Or," Antonia added, "switch them off."

"What do you mean?"

"I distinctly heard the light switched off as I knocked at the door."

"Darling, are you sure you weren't walking in your sleep? This does sound a little odd, you know. No one's been in that wing since we opened the house. The rooms aren't even furnished. They're all dust."

"Then why did Gussie say someone was naughty last night?" Antonia asked triumphantly.

"Gussie!" said Iris. She began to laugh. "Oh, I'm afraid he meant me. I scolded him. He'd been out on the rocks fishing instead of mowing lawns. He's the one who was naughty. But it would be just like him to say it was me. He doesn't like me very much because I expect him to work harder than he's ever done in all his lazy life. He *is* a scamp, that boy."

"So you don't believe there was a light in that room," Antonia persisted.

"Well, actually, dear, I'm afraid I don't. Did you take an aspirin like I told you to?"

"Aspirins don't give me hallucinations."

"Of course they don't. But I think that long trip from England has tired you badly. I mean, there was that odd business in Auckland, too,

78

wasn't there? And you have been ill, haven't you?"

Antonia felt the angry blood rising in her cheeks. Did Iris genuinely believe she was having these blanks, or was she deliberately refusing to believe anything else? She clenched her hands under the table, with an effort controlling herself. Something told her that she mustn't lose her temper now. If she got too upset everyone might end by really convincing her that she was having hallucinations, that no one had ever spoken to her on the telephone in Auckland and that last night she had only dreamed she had walked up those cold draughty stairs and tapped at the door under which a chink of light showed.

"I'll show you over the empty rooms myself if you're not convinced," Iris said, with a look of amusement in her eyes. "You really are a suspicious creature. What do you think we're hiding? A ghost?"

At that moment there was a loud whistling in the hall and Simon came stamping in, his face ruddy from the exertion of his climb up the hill.

"Good morning, girls," he said. "Whew, it's hot!" He came over to Iris, and she held up her cool pointed face for his kiss. "How are you, Tonia? Sleep well?" He didn't wait for her answer. Already his eyes were slipping away evasively. "You carry on with your meal. I've got to feed the birds and then Dougal Conroy wants to see me at his office. First thing, he said."

"Oh," said Iris in sudden interest. Then she said, "Oh, but Simon, you can't this morning. Antonia's coming into town with me to buy a hat and I want you to be here to see those workmen. You know the ones who were supposed to come yesterday. I telephoned and they're coming for sure this morning. Mr. Conroy's business will have to wait until this afternoon."

"He said it was urgent," Simon pointed out.

"I'm sorry about that, but this is a little more urgent. Isn't it, Antonia? After all, it is my wedding hat."

"I thought you'd bought that," said Simon. "That one with the feather."

"Oh, *no*, darling. That's for travelling. I specially wanted Antonia to be with me before I bought the hat I'm being married in."

Simon looked perplexed, his lower lip drooping.

"All right, love, but I don't see what all the fuss is about. Only half a dozen people to see you."

Iris lifted up her arms. Her face was beguiling.

"But you, my sweet. Isn't a bridegroom always expected to remember how his bride looked?"

Simon grinned happily.

"I'd do that anyway, silly. Well, I'd better ring Conroy. I say, a chap down at the hotel knows where I can get some pure white lovebirds. They're quite rare. I'm seeing about them next week. How are you girls getting to town?"

"Oh, order a taxi for us, will you, darling? In an hour's time. And we won't be back until after lunch, so get Bella to give you something. By the way, Simon, Antonia thinks we have a ghost."

Simon couldn't conceal his start of surprise — or was it dismay?

"In the empty wing," Iris went on amusedly. "I don't blame her for thinking it. There are enough odd noises here at night. But they're all perfectly explainable." She turned to Antonia. "I didn't mean you to see the rest of the place until after the alterations had started, but if you won't be convinced it's empty, come and we'll see it now."

In a state of complete bewilderment Antonia rose to follow Iris. She only half registered the fact that Simon was sucking in his full lips in an expression of unbelief, either at her believing in ghosts, or at Iris blithely intending to throw open all the doors in the house and display their secrets.

Iris was going to find one door locked. Perhaps she truly knew nothing about this and would be taken by surprise.

Antonia followed her across the hall and through the door that led up the dusty uncovered stairway to the closed rooms above. Simon was coming behind, breathing heavily as he climbed the stairs. Iris went lightly ahead, chatting animatedly.

"These stairs are going to take acres of carpet. We want all the passages carpeted, too. The place won't echo so much then. It's these high ceilings that throw back the sound. We'll open these doors, Simon, because I want you to show the builders all the rooms when they come." She reached the passage at the head of the stairs and went quickly from door to door, turning the knobs and throwing the doors open. The knob of the third door turned as easily as the rest. The room revealed was exactly the same as the others, empty, dusty, echoing.

"Which was the room you thought you heard sounds in, Antonia?" Iris called.

Antonia looked uncertainly one way and the other. Had she made a mistake? Was it the door on the other side of the passage? But that was open, too, revealing another empty room.

"It was this one," she said, stepping over the threshold.

There was dust on the mantelpiece, the window ledges and the floor. Straws and feathers of old birds' nests littered the fireplace. The high windows were fast shut. The room had a completely desolate, unlived-in look.

Antonia looked bewilderedly from Iris to Simon. Simon's mouth hung open as if he were bewildered, too. But then his mouth always drooped a little. That didn't mean a thing. Neither did the faint shine of perspiration on his forehead which lingered from his climb up the hill.

Iris's brows were raised gently.

"Well, Antonia? Are you satisfied now? Do we have a haunted room?"

"You must," Antonia burst out. "I'll swear there was a light in here last night." She looked at Simon appealingly. "When I tapped on the door it went out."

Simon looked startled. Then his eyes slid away.

"Were you sleep-walking?" he asked.

Iris slipped her arm around Antonia.

"I think she must have been. She was very tired. And as I said this house has a sound system all of its own. Antonia, I think while Simon and I are away on our honeymoon you'd better stay at an hotel. I meant to suggest that, anyway. We're only going for a long week-end, because truly I can't bear to leave here. There's so much to do. But I think you'll be too lonely by yourself."

"Do you think I'm scared or not to be trusted?" Antonia asked.

"Don't be an idiot, darling. I'm only thinking of how lonely you could be. And if you *should* sleep-walk—"

Antonia turned on her fiercely.

"I wasn't sleep-walking as you know very well. You're playing a trick on me."

Iris's face was full of astonishment.

"A trick? But, darling, what on earth *for?*"

# VII

Miss Fox, as usual, intercepted Dougal when he tried to slide unobtrusively into his office in the morning. Nine o'clock was not the time to be brisk and intelligent, and Miss Fox, with her starched snowy collars, her bright eyes snapping behind their black-rimmed glasses, her quick nervous capable hands, always gave the impression of expecting intelligence of an impossibly high order.

"Ah, good morning, Miss Fox," he said resignedly. "Is there anything important?"

"Mr. Mildmay can't get in until the afternoon. He has builders or someone coming this morning. I told him it was important, but he said this was, too."

"That's all right, Miss Fox." Dougal had slept on the amazing information in yesterday's mail, and he was growing more phlegmatic about it. The news would keep until this afternoon.

"But there was this," said Miss Fox, handing him a letter. It was written on plain notepaper in a difficult angular hand. It read simply:

"Has anyone thought it worth while finding out a little of the past life of the woman Iris Matthews who is about to be married to a client of yours, Mr. Simon Mildmay?"

There was no signature. That was all there was to the extraordinary communication.

"What the hell is this?" Dougal exploded. "Who does he — or she — think we are? A detective agency?"

"I would rather think, from the handwriting," Miss Fox suggested primly, "that a doctor may have written that. It's exactly like the writing in all prescriptions I've ever seen."

"Now, Miss Fox, what self-respecting doctor would stoop to anonymous letters?"

"But this is hardly an anonymous letter in the ordinary sense. It sounds as if it's written by someone who suspects something, but wants some verification, so to speak, before he makes himself known. In other words, he feels his suspicions are preposterous but that they shouldn't be dismissed entirely."

Dougal listened to the involved interpretation Miss Fox produced. He tapped his desk irritably with a letter opener.

"For heaven's sake, what is there to suspect? If Simon Mildmay wants to marry a woman with a past that's his pigeon. He might enjoy it — more interesting — Sorry, Miss Fox, that's only a conjecture. But I don't see why we should worry unduly about Simon Mildmay. He's doing all right for himself."

"I wasn't thinking of him so much as the residuary legatee."

Sometimes Miss Fox's meticulous legal language was intensely irritating. Then one caught a gleam in those sharp eyes of hers and suspected she was using it for some deliberate purpose of her own. Dougal had an uncomfortable feeling that she was running his life.

"What has Antonia Webb got to do with it?" he snapped.

"I truly don't know. But I must admit that that letter has made me feel uneasy. After all, who are these people?"

"They're merely clients. We wind up this estate for them and then wave them goodbye."

"You'll never wave them goodbye. You'll have this estate on your hands all your life." Then Miss Fox said outrageously, "Is Miss Webb attractive?"

What was the woman up to? Was she marrying him off, too? This was absurd, these women living his life for him.

"Very," he said shortly. "But that's entirely beside the point. Bring in your book and we'll do some work."

"I was thinking," said Miss Fox, "that the best way to begin with would be to contact someone who travelled to New Zealand on the same ship as Miss Mildmay and Miss Matthews. I understand they met on shipboard. Since it's only six months ago we ought to be able to do that. I'd suggest writing to the shipping company for a copy of the passenger list." She caught Dougal's eye. "I would say that that is entirely within the province of a solicitor who acts in the real interests of his clients."

"Perhaps while you're about it," Dougal said scathingly, "you'll help my mother to solve why there's a light at nights in the unused wing of the Hilltop."

Miss Fox's eyes sparkled.

"Is there? I say, I wonder—" She stopped firmly. "I'm not just inquisitive, Mr. Conroy, as you seem to think. I think this is a most unusual case and we should be prepared for any sort of development." She paused, then added hurriedly, "I'll get my shorthand book."

The development that they were all looking

for, of course, being his falling in love with Antonia Webb, Dougal thought tiredly.

"By the way," he said as Miss Fox returned, "what's *your* first name?"

To his surprise she blushed bright pink.

"Brenda," she said primly.

Thinking with some amusement over the curious phenomenon of Miss Fox's blush and that it was the only way he had been able to get under her composure, Dougal again had a period of obtuseness, and didn't think about the man of whom Antonia had complained, or of the one he had seen with his own eyes getting out of a taxi and staring up the road to the Hilltop.

But when he did remember that he wondered if that person were the mysterious letter writer. What was he doing — trying to create mischief? Or was there genuinely something very much wrong?

Pondering, Dougal decided to take Miss Fox's advice. He would instruct her to find someone who had travelled on the same ship as Iris Matthews and Laura Mildmay.

# VIII

A subtle change seemed to have come over Iris since their return from their shopping expedition. Perhaps it was the purchase of the scrap of tulle and roses that called itself a hat and that became her wonderfully well. Almost every woman enjoyed a frivolous expensive hat. But would the pleasure of it be sufficient to make Iris relax and glow as she was now doing? Or was the change in her due to the fact that now it was almost her wedding day and everything was in order? Or was it from satisfaction because Simon said the builders had been at last and were preparing an estimate for the cost of renovations.

Whatever it was, her tendency to sharpness had completely vanished and she was as soft and charming as a well-fed kitten. Antonia began to understand why Simon had fallen in love with her.

She showed Antonia her trousseau clothes and talked with more frankness than she had yet shown.

"Do you know, this is going to be the first real home I've ever had. That's why I'm so excited about it. My father died when I was very young and my mother – moved about a good deal."

Momentarily her face hardened. Antonia guessed there had been a good deal of hardship in the moving about.

Then Iris flashed a quick smile as if she were regretting her frankness.

"That's when I decided that some day I'd get the kind of place I wanted. I've lived in an awful lot of hotels, most of them not first class. I decided one day I'd own one."

"Wasn't that rather ambitious?" Antonia asked.

"I suppose it was. But one gets what one wants – if one tries hard enough." Again her face was curiously tense. Then she dismissed her thoughts and said brightly, "Do you think Simon will like me in this hat?"

"Simon would like you in anything."

"Yes. Isn't he sweet the way he's crazy about me," Iris said with some smugness.

Antonia pursued the previous subject.

"Tell me, why didn't you look for a place in Auckland?"

Iris was bending over a drawer taking out underclothing.

"Oh, we didn't like Auckland. It was too hot. And your poor aunt was ill at the time. That prejudiced me about the place. I couldn't get away quickly enough after the funeral."

Antonia had a sudden vivid memory of waiting in that small rather dirty café for the owner of a deep husky voice that had sounded at the same time sinister and concerned. All at once she was uneasy again. That incident shouldn't have been dismissed so lightly. No one had the right to do that without making some enquiries about it. If it had really happened, as of course it had, it wouldn't end there. Otherwise why had the stranger bothered to telephone at all?

Simon arrived home at four o'clock. He came hurrying in, and for once omitted to stop in the hall to speak to his birds.

"Iris!" he called through the house. "Iris!"

Iris went quickly to the head of the stairs. It seemed as if the urgency of Simon's voice had startled her. She was a bundle of nerves, Antonia thought. That was hardly to be wondered at if she had nursed a dying woman for several months. Poor thing, she deserved all she was getting.

"I want to talk to you," called Simon.

She ran downstairs and Antonia went to look out of the window of her room. The yellow sunlight was streaming in. The afternoon was warm and golden, the hills, burnt dry of grass, showing their bare bones, the narrow road winding down to the shining roofs of Sumner, the sea curving in a fleece of foam round the bay. Down there Gussie was on the rocks fishing. Iris had sent him. She had been sorry for her sharp temper before breakfast and had said that since the weather was so fine he might as well have the day off to pursue his passionately adored hobby of fishing. After all he was only a child. One couldn't expect a child to work too hard. (Perhaps, Antonia thought, she was remembering her own hard childhood.) Bella was clattering dishes in the kitchen, the birds were keeping up their incessant miniature chatter in the hall. Iris and Simon had gone into the dining-room and closed the door. Antonia wasn't curious about their discussion. But suddenly she was realising that for the first time today she was alone. This would be the time to take another look at that puzzling room in the empty wing where last night someone had cried.

She went quickly and softly down the stairs and across the hall through the connecting door. She wasn't afraid. It was daylight and the doors were all open. Anyway, the builders had been today. They would have noticed if there was anything odd.

Sunlight came in a chink beneath the drawn blind of the empty room. Antonia stealthily raised the blind a few inches so as to see better. She still couldn't reconcile herself to the fact that the room was without furniture, without anything at all that gave a clue as to its last night's occupant.

There were footmarks in the dust on the floor, but they would have been made by herself and Iris this morning, and later the builders. She stooped to touch the dust and noticed that it was mingled with sand. That was a little odd. There was no sand this high up on the hill. It could have been spilt, of course. But how? Who would spill sand accidentally? If it were accidentally. Well, it must be, she told herself, because no one would put it there deliberately. Why should they?

She ran her finger along the mantelpiece and looked at it critically. It was grey with dust — or sand again, for there was sediment in it, and to it clung a hair. A long grey hair.

Antonia shook it off distastefully. Then she picked it up, looking at it thoughtfully. It was eleven or twelve inches long and curled slightly.

The kind of hair one could imagine an elderly woman twisting into a bob.

But no elderly woman lived at the Hilltop, certainly no woman with grey hair. Iris's was pale gold, her own red. Even Bella hadn't a sign of grey in her head.

Of course it could have been left there from the last occupant when the Hilltop still took guests. But Iris had said the house had stood empty for six months, and before that a family had lived there. There were still the relics of the sandpit and the swings in the garden to show that children had been there.

Without knowing why, Antonia was quite certain the rather morbid relic she had discovered had been left there very recently. She remembered Gussie's information, "She were naughty last night." Iris had said he had referred to her. But Iris hadn't cried and rattled the window in the night. Then who had it been?

Standing in the silent room Antonia had a distinct feeling of fear. As if that crying voice were very close to her and asking for help. It was uncanny and extremely unpleasant. She thought rapidly of whom she could ask for help — if help were required.

Dougal Conroy was the obvious choice, but he wouldn't believe this story any more than he had the one about her bags being searched in Auckland. She knew at once that he was too practical and prosaic, perhaps as a defence against his mother's tendency to have flights of imagination. If Dougal were to help her she would have to produce some tangible evidence of trouble.

So there was no one — except that unexplained voice over the telephone offering to tell her about Aunt Laura's death, that frightening voice with its odd threat.

It was disturbing that it was of that which she thought while she stood in this peculiar haunted room with the ownerless grey hair from a human head in her hand.

Simon and Iris were still shut in the dining room. Antonia made a sudden decision and went downstairs to the kitchen. Iris had shown this room to her yesterday. It was a big old-fashioned room with an electric stove in the wide mouth of the chimney where once a coal range had been. There was a table in the middle of the room, and there, it seemed, Bella was usually to be found, mixing puddings or preparing vegetables, her little round-backed figure stooping over the dishes.

She was there now, her figure obscured in a large floral apron, her thin face with its tired lines bent over the pile of peas that she was shelling. When Antonia came in she looked up with a quick uneasy expression in her eyes.

"Are you wanting something, Miss? If it's Gussie he's had an accident and I've sent him to bed."

"What did he do?"

"He fell off those rocks where he goes fishing. Might have been drowned, but he will go out that far." She added quickly, "Miss Matthews gave him permission to go fishing today. It was very kind of her.'

Antonia guessed that Gussie was a source of worry and grief to his mother. She looked as if he gave her sleepless nights.

"No, Bella, I don't want Gussie. I came to see you. Since we're living in the same house we ought to get acquainted."

Bella didn't answer. She wasn't a talkative woman and she still looked suspicious.

"How is your husband?" Antonia asked.

"Just the same, Miss. But I think—" Suddenly a lighting up, a kind of faded sweetness, came into Bella's thin face. "I think I'm getting him out of hospital into a convalescent home at last. That way he'll get well. He was so fed up of hospital, it was making him worse."

"That's fine," said Antonia sympathetically.

"And as soon as he's well enough he can come here, Miss Matthews says."

Antonia was moved by Iris's kindness. The knowledge of that removed some of the vague uneasiness about Iris herself in her mind.

"That's nice for you, Bella. You must have had a worrying time with him ill for so long."

Obviously this was the way to Bella's heart, and to her tongue.

"It's Gussie being such a scamp," she burst out. "I do try to manage him, but he just seems naturally bad. I wouldn't have liked being up here, it's that lonely, if Miss Matthews hadn't been so good about having Gussie here. It's not everyone would put up with a bad boy like that. And the air's so good for him. He's been threatened with his father's trouble, you know. That's why he's missed a lot of school. I think if he had more learning he'd be a better boy. It's just that he's got nothing in his mind to think about but mischief."

Antonia felt sorry for the thin troubled woman, even if she did think privately that Gussie had inherited his sly foxy look from his mother.

"It is lonely here, isn't it." At last she was getting round to the subject she had wanted to open. "Do you know, last night I could have sworn there was someone in the empty wing."

Did Bella's face change? Did it grow more narrow and secretive? That must be her imagination. For Bella was looking at her and saying:

"Oh, you'd be mistaken, Miss. There ain't no one there. It's that whistling buoy that gets on your nerves at night. If you ask me it's a funny place for a guest house, so far from the beach and all."

"Gussie said—"

"Now don't you pay any attention to Gussie, Miss. He's a fair terror for telling lies. I'm only waiting till his father's well enough to manage him. No, it would be seagulls, Miss. And that buoy."

"But the light," Antonia murmured. "There was a light."

Did Bella's voice falter?

"If there was a light it would likely be Miss Matthews. She goes about dreaming how she's going to fix up those rooms. Night or day, it's the same to her." She paused to let her small faded eyes rest on Antonia. "Unless you were sleep-walking, Miss."

"No," said Antonia violently. "I wasn't."

"Wasn't you, Miss? I wouldn't know how you'd rightly know about that. Now if you'll excuse me I'll have to get the dinner on."

If the explanation were that Iris herself were walking about why hadn't Iris told her? But Iris hadn't got grey hair. That was her first triumphant clue.

Going back through the hall Antonia heard the telephone ringing. It was in a little alcove under the stairs. Since no one came to answer it Antonia went and picked up the receiver.

"Hullo," she said lightly.

"Is that the Hilltop?" came a slow thick voice.

Antonia tensed. That voice! It was unmistakable.

"Yes, this is the Hilltop," she got out. Her voice sounded calm enough. It didn't indicate the way her heart was beating and her mouth growing dry.

"I would like to speak to Miss Matthews, if you please."

It was Iris he wanted! What business had he with Iris who already knew all about Aunt Laura's death?

Antonia put the receiver down with a clatter, her rigid fingers unclenching from it.

"Who is it, Tonia?" she heard Iris calling. "Someone for me?"

"Yes. Yes, it's for you."

But who was it? *Who?*

No one, Antonia argued, under those circumstances, could have walked out of the hall and not listened to Iris's half of the conversation.

Antonia poked her finger through the wire of the bird cage, letting the honey-coloured bird nibble at it and whisper in its intimate voice.

She heard Iris saying, "Who?" sharply. Then, in a violent whisper, "Wait a minute!" As if recollecting herself her voice changed again. She said in a businesslike manner, "I have the plans upstairs. Wait till I go and get them."

Antonia knew that she would continue the conversation from the telephone in her bedroom. She had rapidly made an excuse to go up there to speak in privacy.

If one were to lift the receiver down here one could hear . . .

"Isn't he a beauty?" came Simon's voice in Antonia's ear, making her start so that the yellow bird fluttered off her finger. Simon thrust his own finger through the wires, crooking it enticingly.

"Come here, come here, you beauty." Then he opened the cage door and letting the bird settle on his finger carefully withdrew it. The bird sidled rapidly up his arm and on to his shoulder. Simon pursed his moist lips, his eyes beaming. "Pretty boy, pretty boy," he cooed. The miniature voice, like a ghostly distorted echo, came back, "Pretty boy, pretty boy!"

The telephone was out of reach now. Antonia could hear the faint crackle of voices in the receiver. She could have burst into tears of angry frustration. There, three yards away, was a clue to the mystery and she couldn't seize it.

Simon oblivious to her despair, was smiling with pleasure. He took the bird on his finger and holding its tiny beak to his mouth made rapturous kissing sounds. Then he said, "Say lucky girl! Lucky girl!" He looked sideways at Antonia. She had a queer feeling that he was meaning her. But surely he must mean Iris. "Lucky girl!" he insisted.

"Simon!" cried Iris in a high taut voice behind them. "Simon don't be so asinine about those damned birds."

A look of hurt surprise came over Simon's face.

"Honey! Honey, you're not jealous?"

"Jealous! Good God!" Iris turned on her heel and flounced towards the kitchen. Antonia caught no more than a glimpse of her tense white face.

"Has something upset you?" Simon called. "Who was ringing?"

"Oh, just a man. Just one of those stupid builders. He's being difficult about materials." She went on out of sight.

"Simon," said Antonia urgently, "I recognised that voice. It was the man who rang me in Auckland."

"What, that mysterious fellow?" Simon's

mouth fell open. "But it couldn't have been. That was one of the builders. Iris just said." He paused to think. He looked puzzled and uneasy. Then he said definitely, "Their voices must have been alike. You could easily mistake a voice over the telephone. He didn't – actually mention Aunt Laura, did he?" he added uneasily.

"No."

Simon's face cleared.

"Then of course, you're imagining it. You've got the jitters. Iris has, too. But Iris has more excuse than you have."

"Why?"

Simon looked at her coyly.

"Doesn't a girl get a bit jittery before her wedding?"

But not Iris, Antonia thought silently. Iris was too sophisticated to let the mere fact of acquiring a husband disturb her poise.

# IX

There was a steep path from the Hilltop down the cliff's edge. It was a path Gussie took when he went fishing, scampering over the dried grass on his bare feet, giving no heed to the steep dangerous drop over the cliff's edge to the jagged rocks beneath. If one went too near the edge the dried earth could so easily crumble. Antonia took that path the next morning, and two hours later climbed up it, swinging her wet swimming suit and looking hot and sunburnt.

Iris was upstairs trying to rest before lunch, Simon said as she went in. He didn't think she was able to rest very much because he could hear her walking about her room.

"I'm glad you'll be here to feed the birds," he said. "Iris said Bella could manage, but I couldn't trust her like I could you. I've shown you where the seed is and you won't forget to change their water, will you? And talk to Johnnie. He likes it. He gets lonely without a little attention."

"I'll remember them," said Antonia. She was impatient to go upstairs and find out why Iris couldn't rest. But would Iris tell her if she asked? She would say, as she had said to Simon, that she was suffering from nerves and not from some peculiar private fear which was associated with the telephone call she had yesterday.

She went to her room to change, and then there came Iris's voice from outside saying:

"Antonia, what extraordinary things you do! Bringing in this horrid wet seaweed."

Antonia went to the door and stared in amazement at the brown dripping seaweed lying on the floor.

"But how did it get there?" she exclaimed. "I didn't bring it."

Iris stooped and picked it up gingerly.

"Darling, you must have. Who else would? But you might have left it outside."

"I didn't!" Antonia insisted. "What would I bring it *for?*"

"I haven't the faintest notion. But there it is, isn't it? And no one else has been to the beach this morning. Not even Gussie."

Iris had on a faded cotton housecoat tied round her thin waist with a cord. She had a cigarette between her lips. Her eyes narrowed against the smoke. She looked nervy, as if an argument would snap the last threads of her patience.

"Take it downstairs, will you," she said, handing the slimy unpleasant stuff to Antonia.

Antonia was suddenly angry.

"You must think I'm an imbecile," she exclaimed. "Walking in my sleep, bringing home this nasty messy stuff for a joke!"

Iris frowned wearily.

"Honestly, darling, I don't know what to think. Let's not worry about it now. Just get rid of that stuff. I've got a splitting head and how I'm going to look like anything but a rag this afternoon I don't know." She patted Antonia's arm. "These things aren't important. I mean, they're just silly, aren't they. But I think you ought to see a doctor. We'll fix it when Simon and I get back after the week-end."

"And what do you think I'm suffering from?" Antonia asked. She wanted to retain her anger, because that way she didn't feel this queer fear, this sense of danger closing round her. If she stayed angry the whole thing was just ridiculous.

"There's something called limited amnesia,"

Iris said. "I'd insist on your going to an hotel while we're away, but Simon says there are his birds. And after all you don't do anything dangerous, do you?" She pressed her hand to her forehead. She had a look of extraordinary tension as if she could well be the person suffering from amnesia.

"Darling, when you take that stuff outside would you bring me up a brandy and water. Mostly brandy." She smiled forlornly. "I didn't know I'd be a jittery bride. Isn't it silly!"

Antonia had a feeling that the stranger with the thick slow voice might come into the church during the marriage ceremony. She kept looking towards the open door and not paying a lot of attention to the minister's murmured words, or to Iris's thin pointed face with its glitter of excitement and tension, or to Simon's large figure, oddly untidy even in his new dark suit. Simon repeated the marriage vows after the minister in an almost absent voice. Simon's mind would be dwelling more on the Song of Solomon — *sweet is thy voice and fair is thy face.* He would be waiting to spend his passion on the unloosed splendour of Iris's hair.

No one else came into the church. There was just herself and Dougal Conroy and Dougal's mother, a large woman with a plain face and bright observant humorous eyes.

Henrietta Conroy, Antonia thought, wouldn't miss much. Did she have the feeling that this marriage was completely unreal?

After the ceremony the five of them went back to the Conroys' house for tea served by a plump heavy-handed maid who was inclined to giggle at any remark at all, and later still Simon and Iris went away in the car hired by Simon for the week-end. Their last remarks to Antonia came back on the rising wind, Iris's "Lock your door at nights, darling, in case you *should* sleep-walk," and Simon's, "Don't forget to change the birds' water each day."

Henrietta Conroy, with her rich warm voice and her constant chatter about everything in the world, had provided the only gaiety there had been at that odd little ceremony. Now, as Iris and Simon left, she turned to Antonia.

"Do you sleep-walk, dear? How interesting."

"I don't," Antonia denied, raising her voice to reach Henrietta's hearing. "At least, I'm sure I don't."

Henrietta looked at her curiously.

"Then why does Iris say you do?"

"Oh — things have happened."

"Things! But you must tell me. Mustn't she, Dougal?"

Dougal frowned.

"Don't take any notice of my mother, Antonia. She's just inquisitive."

"And why shouldn't I be?" Henrietta retorted. "It isn't a crime. Tell me, *who* sleeps in the empty wing? I understood it wasn't being used at all."

"Why do you ask that?" Antonia enquired sharply.

"Well, someone keeps awfully late hours. I see a light burning at three o'clock in the morning."

"Then there *is* one," Antonia said triumphantly. "That was one thing Iris said I must have imagined. But do you know the room's absolutely empty. Absolutely. Dust everywhere."

"How very odd! Isn't it, Dougal?"

"There's probably an explanation, mother."

"Of course there is. There's an explanation to everything. But it's such fun finding it. Dougal says I have a distorted imagination, Antonia. Do you think your cousin is hiding someone up there?"

"But the room's empty," Antonia repeated. "I saw it. Except for that grey hair I picked up, of course."

"A grey hair!" Henrietta pounced on the information eagerly. "I knew it! Your Aunt Laura has been murdered for her money."

"Mother!" Dougal remonstrated. "Don't be

absurd. Laura Mildmay died in Auckland on the first of last month."

Henrietta sagged disappointedly.

"Then it's someone else."

"No one at all has been murdered. Don't talk such nonsense. The grey hair will belong to a cleaning woman. It could have been there for months."

Henrietta looked sadly at Antonia.

"My son has no imagination. He makes life so ordinary. It's that woman he's got at the office. That Miss Fox."

"What's wrong with her?" Dougal asked mildly.

"She's too efficient. You've said so yourself. Life can be ruined by efficiency. Can't it, Ethel?"

The stout maid who had come in to gather up the dishes gave a deep-throated giggle. She didn't speak. To Antonia she gave the impression of never speaking. She thought of Dougal surrounded by the efficient Miss Fox, the giggling Ethel and his mother with her mind full of fantastic weavings. No wonder he was so reserved and practical. If odd things happened to him he just wouldn't believe them. He would let people tell him he had been suffering from limited amnesia. Or would he? He might be very much more stubborn than that. She was aware of a great curiosity to find out what he was really like. Her eyes suddenly began to twinkle with mischief. She wouldn't let him drive her home but would suggest walking up the hill in the growing darkness. And she would make him kiss her. Just for fun.

Antonia Webb, you're being a little miss! she told herself. Perhaps she was. But the mischievous desire to feel Dougal Conroy's lips against hers persisted.

The wind bent the tamarisk tree at the gate and sent its lonely rustling up and down the hillside. The sky was champagne coloured, the hills were drawing shadows like blankets over their bony ridges. Down in Sumner the white houses perched in tiers on the steep sheltered cliffs, the gay pink and yellow portulacca and geraniums ran riot in the gardens. The sea drifted in and out over the sand in gentle wavelets, reserving its wildness for the dark rocks on the other side of the hill. No sound of the melancholy whistling buoy came down into this sheltered valley.

Henrietta called goodnight to them from the open doorway.

"You should stay here," she called. "If anything frightens you be sure to ring up and Dougal will come and get you."

Dougal, rather stiffly, put his arm through

111

hers. She drew closer to him companionably. As they climbed the wind grew colder and stronger. The thorny bleak manuka bushes crouched like giant spiders against the hillside.

"Are you going to be nervous up there?" Dougal asked politely. "Don't let my mother's nonsense worry you."

What about her own 'nonsense' Antonia wondered. She had talked as much as Henrietta had.

"No, I don't think so," she answered quite honestly. After all, nothing had happened. It had all been sound, the voice on the telephone, the voice crying in the night, the window rattling, the snap of the light going off. It was a subtle assault on her ears, but nothing had actually happened. The evidence of one's ears was neither tangible nor visible.

"It might have been wise for you to stay in an hotel," Dougal said. He added, "Or with us." Antonia had the impression that he would prefer her in an hotel. She shook her head.

"Bella and Gussie are there. And Simon wants me to look after his birds. No, I'll be perfectly all right. After all, I know that room is empty."

"Of course it is," Dougal said. His voice was a little puzzled. "It's odd, though. There was a light, you know. I saw it myself. But there must be a simple explanation for it."

"Then why doesn't someone make it?"

She contemplated telling him about Iris's curious telephone call yesterday, then decided against it. She didn't want to be scoffed at again for making a mountain out of a molehill. This, she divined, was something she was going to have to work out alone. Besides, she didn't want to talk about it now. They were a man and a woman walking home alone and she had this odd inquisitive desire to rouse him to a little warmth. In the past her chief trouble had been to moderate the warmth of male approaches. Dougal Conroy intrigued her by his aloofness. But it was probably defensive. Poor boy, he was smothered by women.

"Never mind about all those things now," she said lightly. "If it's a nice day will you come swimming with me tomorrow?"

She felt him stiffen slightly.

"Tomorrow? Well—"

"Ah, come now, don't say you can't," Antonia exclaimed. She was still being mischievous, but she found the thought of lazing on the sand with this fair-headed reserved young man pleasant. She was a little lonely after all.

"I usually go fishing at week-ends," he said. "With a friend. Up country. We get salmon in one of the rivers."

Antonia could see him then, in waders and a sports jacket, his fair hair blown by the mountain winds, his eyes blue and keen. She felt lonelier.

"You don't like women, do you?"

She felt him give an impatient movement.

"You have no reason to say that."

"Haven't I? Perhaps I should define it and say you don't like the sort of women who come bouncing all the way from England to grab a legacy." She stopped being facetious. She couldn't think why she was behaving so stupidly, and added, "It wasn't the money that brought me. It was what I felt Aunt Laura had really left me – her love for travel and adventure. I felt I was letting her down if I didn't accept the challenge."

Dougal said nothing for a moment. They were almost at the top of the hill. Bella had left the hall light on and the house lifted its spare white shape with its one eye shining yellow.

Then Dougal removed his arm from hers and said, "You shouldn't have come. There was no need for you to come."

Antonia felt completely rebuffed.

"Oh, that's unkind."

He made an impulsive movement. It was too dark to see his face, but she could sense his earnestness.

"There was nothing personal in that. I assure you there wasn't."

Antonia laughed. His earnestness was amusing and rather endearing. Obscurely she felt he was her ally, even though in a hostile and disapproving kind of way.

"Well, why did you say it?"

They had reached the door and her hand was on the knob. She had forgotten her early determination to have him kiss her. The moment wouldn't come now. She realised that he would not take his kisses lightly – odder still she would dislike it if he did.

"You know," he burst out, "it will be a good thing when you've had that birthday and get possession of your capital."

"Why ever do you say that?" Now she was astonished. "Do you think Simon isn't to be trusted? *I'm* perfectly happy about him. Anyway, he isn't particularly interested in money and it would take more than four thousand pounds to make him go wrong. Don't be fanciful."

Dougal didn't answer. She opened the door and the light fell across his face. She saw its seriousness and suddenly she was touched.

"It *is* nice of you to worry about my interests. I appreciate it even if I don't seem to. Thank you for bringing me home."

He hesitated. "Are you sure you'll be all right?"

"Of course. I promise to ring if I'm not."

"Do that. I'll come right up."

She laughed again. "You won't need to, of course. You really are getting fanciful."

But as she shut the door she knew she was wrong. Dougal Conroy was never fanciful. She stood a moment in the hall reflecting on what he had said. Something must have been worrying him to cause him to make a statement like that. But what could it be? He was catching the jitters from the rest of them, that was all.

The birds were asleep, the curtain drawn across their cage. Without their twitter the hall seemed oppressively silent. Antonia looked up the dark stairway. She would go to her room and go straight to bed. "Lock your door," Iris had said. But that was nonsense. She didn't sleep-walk. Or did she? How would she know that she didn't? How would she know she hadn't brought that seaweed into the house this morning? If she did suffer from amnesia she would be unaware of it. That was where the whole thing became a vicious circle.

The wind battered at the side of the house. It seemed to be rising. Antonia listened intently to see if a window rattled. None did. Yet the wind was stronger now than it had been last night. How queer. Nothing made sense. She was too tired now to reflect any more about it. Bed was the best place.

She went upstairs slowly, switching on the light on the upper floor and switching off the one in the hall. The windows of her room were open and the curtains billowed in. The room was full of the smell of the sea. As she went to close the windows a fine spray blew in her face. It was a misty rain come suddenly over the top of the hill. She remembered that she had left her swimming suit and some other washing on the line. Bella may have brought them in, but if she hadn't they would be blown to pieces. She would have to go down and see.

When she opened the back door the wind blew full against her, nearly making her lose her balance. At the bottom of the lawn she could see the ghostly shapes of her clothing flapping madly. She ran across the grass to rescue it. Her nightdress had got caught in the spiky foliage of a toi toi bush. The sword leaves crackled as she reached for it, and the feathery plumes brushed against her cheek. She gathered all her clothing in her arms and turned with relief to the house. The back door had blown shut and no light showed. Above the outline of the roof dark clouds raced, showing brief intervals of light colourless sky. The sound of the whistling buoy was clear and strong and melancholy.

What a place to build a house, she thought, struggling back across the lawn. She hoped the door didn't lock automatically when it shut.

Then it occurred to her that she hadn't heard it bang. *Could* the wind have shut it? But of course it could. How else would it have shut? The sound of its closing would be carried away from her. It had probably woken Bella who would get up to see what was happening.

At that moment Antonia hurried up the path to the door and turned the knob. It turned easily and the next moment she was inside. How silly she was to get so panicky. There was no sign of Bella who couldn't have been awakened after all. The passage into the hall and the hall itself was quite empty.

Yet it was at that moment that Antonia had the sensation of being watched.

She couldn't explain it. Everything was still. No shadow had moved. No footsteps had sounded. Yet she could have sworn that from some point of vantage two eyes were watching her.

The first prickles of fear ran over her scalp. She stood still, holding her breath, trying to listen. But the night sounds outside defeated her. The heavy gusts of wind, the distant thunder of the sea, the staccato crackle of the flaxbush, drowned any small sound that there might be within the house.

If she were being watched she had to show the watcher that she was not afraid. She summoned all her nonchalance to cross over to the bird cage and draw back the curtains a fraction to see if the birds were all right.

The lemon-coloured bird moved its feet and whispered sleepily.

"Pretty boy!" Antonia murmured.

Without turning, she speculated on how far away the telephone was. It was in the alcove under the stairs. She would have to cross the hall to reach it. The alcove was dark. It might well be her watcher's hiding place — if there were a watcher. Anyway, how could she ring the Conroys at this stage when nothing at all had happened? She could call Bella, but again what was there to tell her? Why frighten her unnecessarily?

She wished uselessly that she had let her clothes tear to ribbons on the line and stayed in the safety of her bedroom.

Well — what was preventing her getting back to her bedroom now? Nothing. The hall was empty, the staircase empty. All she had to do was traverse the short distance upstairs and along the passage to her door. In less than a minute she would be there. Only she mustn't hurry too much in case whoever might be in the house would scorn her faint-heartedness.

With a firm footstep she crossed the hall and began to climb the stairs.

Did someone creep out to follow her? She didn't know. She didn't look round. She reached the top of the stairs and then covered the remaining distance to her room in a dozen quick steps.

As she closed the door she heard Iris's voice in her memory, "Lock your door, darling." But that was in case she should sleep-walk, not because there might be an intruder in the house. Now, trying to catch her breath, she did turn the key in the lock. She also shut the windows and drew the curtains across, first glancing to see that there was no light in the empty wing.

A few minutes later, when she had smoked a cigarette and quietened her nervous trembling, she began to get back her sense of proportion. Of course there had been no one in the hall. She had let her imagination run away with her. She had got into a panic and turned shadows into people. Who on earth would have been watching her? It couldn't even have been the occupant of the empty room because there was no occupant. She had assured herself of that. It was Iris who had switched the light on there for purposes of her own. Tonight Iris was away so there would be no light.

But Iris hadn't got grey hair....

Antonia began, firmly, to undress. She wouldn't even yield to an old-maidish desire to look under the bed. If anyone were hiding in the house at least they would have the good sense not to hide in her room. Besides, there wasn't anyone. Bella would have heard them if there had been. It was the wind that had blown the door shut.

In the pretty room Iris had so thoughtfully prepared for her there was even a selection of new books. Antonia chose an anthology of poetry and got into bed.

With the windows closed the sound of the wind and sea was muffled. There were no gulls crying, no windows rattling. The house was quite peaceful.

Antonia read resolutely. Her eyelids were drooping. She had come to New Zealand after an illness. It was not a good thing to go to bed emotionally exhausted as she seemed to be doing. She must shut problems and imaginary fears out of her mind.

*Sleep with the lily hands has passed him by,* she read sadly.

She closed the book and leaned over to put out the light. In the same instant the front

door shut. Not loudly, but louder than someone had meant it to. As if, at the last minute, the
wind had blown it out of his hand. Or her hand.

*Who was it?*

Antonia forced herself to get out of bed and
peer through a chink in the curtains at the dark
garden. There was no moon and it was too dark
to see. Even had someone stood on the lawn
directly in front of her window she could
scarcely have seen him. The toi toi moved its
luminous plumes against the sky. Nothing but
the flaxbush and the young pines and the toi
toi plumes moved.

She was almost crying, biting her lips to keep
back her sobs. Whoever had been in the house
had gone without doing any harm, but it wasn't
fair that she should not be allowed to sleep.

All these noises — as if someone was trying
to wear her out through the medium of her
ears. She longed for the deafness of Henrietta
Conroy, the blessed boon of silence.

Nothing would induce her to leave her room.
In any case, what purpose would it serve? The
bird had flown.

But sleep had flown, too. She lit another cigarette and thought desolately of brandy in hot
milk, or just a good cup of tea. Maybe later she
would have enough courage to go down to the
kitchen.

It was nearly midnight. In six hours it would be daylight. She would sleep all day tomorrow if she wished. Even now what had happened was not real or serious enough to make it necessary to telephone the Conroys. She couldn't bring Dougal up the hill just to tell him that perhaps Bella had had a visitor.

That's who it would be — a visitor Bella didn't want anyone to see. Probably he had only been asked because Iris and Simon were away. Why hadn't she thought of that before? Antonia wondered, in intense relief. Now she could go back to bed and sleep, even without the aid of hot milk.

She climbed back into bed, drawing the covers over her and wearily relaxing. It was impossible to tell how much later it was that the telephone rang.

Antonia started up from a deep sleep and automatically scrambled out of bed. Who would be ringing at this hour? It must be serious. She would have to answer the telephone. Anyway, her drowsy mind told her, the intruder had gone. It was quite safe.

With her wrap half pulled on and her feet in bedroom slippers she opened the door and ran along the passage to the stairs.

It was half way down the stairs that she slipped. She was perfectly conscious of doing that, and of snatching wildly for the banister before she fell. In a split second her mind registered panic. And someone screamed. Then there was nothing at all....

# X

"Dougal," Henrietta Conroy called in her resonant voice, "you'll have to go up to the Hilltop."

Dougal, starting from a sound sleep, sat up in alarm.

"What's wrong?"

"I hope nothing is. But the hall light's still on and it's four o'clock."

"Mother, don't you ever sleep?" Dougal said with weary exasperation. "I expect they've just forgotten to switch it off."

"My dear boy, it was off. It went on at three o'clock and it's been on ever since."

Dougal put one leg out of bed.

"Does one interfere?" he said doubtfully. "Antonia might have a visitor."

"At four o'clock in the morning? Antonia isn't that sort of girl." Henrietta's voice was definite. "It's more likely she's been murdered."

Dougal rather hastily let his other leg follow the first.

"Rubbish, Mother! That preposterous imagination of yours—"

"Though the car did go away a little after midnight," Henrietta went on reflectively, "and after that the lights were off."

"What car? Who was up there?" Dougal was pulling on his trousers.

"Darling, how should I know? I just saw the headlights coming down the road."

"It may have been someone looking at the view, or making love," Dougal shouted.

"It well may. Or it may have been someone kidnapping Antonia."

Dougal struggled into his shirt.

"Who would want to kidnap her, for goodness sake?"

"Practically anyone. She's very attractive. So alive. So adventurous and brave."

"Who likes adventurous women?" Dougal muttered. He was remembering his conversation with Antonia earlier, and didn't think he was particularly interested in whether she had been kidnapped or not. She deserved it, a woman with so definite a mind. She deserved that thick red hair of hers to be sharply pulled for being so impulsive and stubborn and running into trouble. He would like to do it himself.

He threw on his overcoat and charged out of the room.

"If she's still alive, poor child," came Henrietta's distressed voice, "bring her down here."

The car had got cold and was slow to start. Dougal had a mind to abandon it and run up the hillside. He stood on the starter again and the engine gave a resigned cough. If Antonia were in any sort of trouble he would have to disregard both Laura Mildmay's and Simon's instructions and tell her the truth. Her aunt had wanted to protect her from fortune hunters, but Simon's reasons for keeping her in ignorance were more disturbing. Iris and he, it appeared, were worried about apparent illusions and absent-minded actions from which Antonia suffered.

"She had this theory that her bags were searched in Auckland," Simon had said earnestly. "Then she thought she heard noises all night, and today, after she'd been swimming, she brought a great lump of seaweed back into the house and swore she hadn't. But there it was lying on the floor making a slimy mess. Iris was very upset. She said if anything more happened she'd persuade Antonia to see a doctor. She'd been ill in London recently, you know." He had looked perplexed, his light blue eyes squeezed within their puffy lids. "We don't think she should stay at the Hilltop alone, but she insists. I only hope she remembers to look after my birds." Then he added, "Iris says a sudden revelation like this might be very bad for her just now, quite apart from Aunt Laura's wishes about it. She ought to get stronger first."

Dougal found it difficult to reconcile that information with Antonia's clear bright eyes and directness of manner. Though he had to admit that one or two of the experiences she had insisted she had had were a little unlikely and far-fetched. Perhaps Iris and Simon who had had a better chance to observe her were right. Perhaps she should be watched.

Anyway, here he was rushing up to the Hilltop at four o'clock in the morning because lights were burning in the windows.

When he stopped the car at the front door and got out and rang the doorbell no one came. He had to ring three times before queer hopping dragging footsteps came across the parquet floor of the hall. Then, for some unknown reason, prickles of apprehension and horror ran over his scalp. Who was going to open the door? Was there something curious and horrible within that walked on one leg and dragged the other? Was Antonia alone with a creature none of them knew anything about? The footsteps had stopped at the door and someone was fumbling with the lock. A great sweep of wind went over the house and the whistling buoy sent its sharp melancholy call, like a trapped bird, up the hill. Dougal wiped the perspiration from his brow. And the door opened.

After all, it was Antonia who stood there. His relief was so great that he burst out laughing at his momentarily truant imagination. Good enough for Henrietta, it had been. Antonia, leaning against the doorpost, was staring at him with oddly dilated eyes.

"What the devil do you think you're laughing at?" she snapped. Then with a movement that seemed half impulse and half collapse she tumbled into his arms.

"Good gracious!" he muttered, supporting her with his arm around her waist. Her slender firm body made him think of one of his beloved fishing rods, beautifully made, firm yet supple, pliant to one's touch, responsive.

She ceased to clutch at him so violently. She sighed deeply and lifted her head to rub her cheek against his. Then it was she who began to laugh, but in a breathless slightly hysterical way.

"Dougal, your cheek's like a kitten's tongue. You know, rough and soft at the same time."

What an extraordinary thing to say! Dougal rubbed his cheek uncomfortably.

"I need a shave. It's almost morning. My mother got into a panic because your light was still on. She made me come up to see if anything was wrong. Why on earth were you walking like that when you came to the door?"

Antonia swayed against him.

"You try walking on a sprained ankle."

He noticed then her pallor and the painful dilation of her eyes.

"Is your ankle sprained?"

"My dear Mr. Conroy — I wouldn't be leaning against you — in the best traditions of melodrama — if it wasn't because my own legs — won't hold—" Her faint ironical voice ceased completely as she slid down at his feet.

He picked her up in his arms. There was nothing else to do. He had to carry her right upstairs to her bedroom because there was nothing to lay her on in the hall that looked like a morgue with its sheeted birds' cage. Anyway, she would have to go upstairs eventually.

As he eased her gently on to the bed she opened her eyes. For a moment they were full of dark panic, the panic through which the poor kid for some reason had been going. Then she realised where she was.

"Did I faint? How extraordinarily silly of

me. It was from relief, I guess."

"What's been happening here tonight?" he demanded.

"You're asking me! The telephone rang and I went to answer it and I fell down the stairs. And someone screamed," she finished, her eyes growing dark again.

"That would be yourself," Dougal said gently.

"No it wouldn't. That was the queer thing. I was too intent on trying to save myself. I caught the banisters and managed to do no more than bump my head and twist my ankle."

Dougal noticed, for the first time, the dark swelling on her forehead.

"Good heavens, you might have been killed!"

"Yes, so I might. Whoever it was who screamed probably thought I was going to be. Probably was disappointed I wasn't."

"Why do you say that?" Dougal asked sharply.

"I don't know. Why did I think there was someone watching me? Why did I hear the front door close, why did the telephone ring, why did I slip?" Now there was a kind of deliberate gaiety in her face. She was still very pale, but she didn't look scared. If she were scared she refused to show it.

"You need a good brandy."

"I'm afraid the brandy's all gone." She smiled wryly. "Go down to the kitchen and see."

"What do you mean?"

"Bella. It must be her weakness. There's an empty bottle on the table and she's in her bed, dead to the world. I got myself out there to see if she could do something for my ankle, and that's what I found. Courvoisier, too."

"Does she pinch it?" Dougal asked.

"Either that or they give it to her."

"You mean Iris and Simon? Good heavens! Why encourage one's cook to drink?"

"Maybe to make her stay. It's lonely here. Or maybe—"

"What?"

She hesitated. Then she said, "Well, it wasn't Bella who screamed."

"It was probably you yourself. In those circumstances one does things one doesn't realise."

She looked at him unbelievingly. She was wearing a peacock blue silk dressing-gown. With the dark flame of her hair and her pale face she had the delicate gay colours of Simon's birds. She was too picturesque for him to feel comfortable with her. Yet the bruise on her forehead, her hurt ankle and her deliberate courage made her seem as if she needed protection. What had he got himself into with his mother's high-flown imagination and this girl's strange exploits?

"Dougal," she was saying, "do you think you

could put a cold compress or something on my ankle? Or try to wake Bella up to do it. It's not so painful now, but if we don't do something I might be tied here, and—"

He knew what she was thinking without her finishing. She wouldn't want to be helpless here with strange things going on. She had to be in possession of all her faculties.

Fortunately he had an elementary knowledge of first aid. He went down to the kitchen to get a basin and to look for materials for a bandage. The first thing he saw was the brandy bottle on the table. He picked it up and turned it upside down. A solitary drop ran out. Bella was a thorough drinker. Well, she had a sick husband and a son who looked as if he would grow up to be an habitual criminal. No one had a better excuse for drinking.

"Fantastic!" he murmured aloud. He gathered his materials, a basin of cold water, towels, a linen tea cloth which he ruthlessly tore up for a bandage. Then he looked into the cocktail cabinet in the lounge and found a whisky bottle with an inch or two of whisky in the bottom. He took that, too, with glasses, and set everything on a tray. With the tray held in front of him he couldn't watch his footstep on the stairs. Half-way up he slid on something and nearly came crashing down with everything he carried. The glasses rattled and the whisky bottle teetered dangerously. He had to set the tray down for a minute to restore the equilibrium of its contents. It was then that he saw the scrap of seaweed, wet, squashy, vilely slippery, lying on the step. He left the tray where it was and picking up the seaweed by one of its brown oozing strands, carried it into Antonia's room.

"Look!" he said simply. "This was on the stairs."

Antonia got on to her elbow.

"Not again!" she whispered. "Iris found some this morning. She swore I had brought it in – in one of my waking trances, I suppose. I'd been down on the beach. I suppose it could have got caught in my bathing suit, or my towel."

"Not this," said Dougal. "This is too wet."

Her widened eyes sought his.

"You mean, it's been put here tonight – by whoever came into the house?"

"Heaven knows!" he said roughly. He was deeply disturbed. The feeling made him angry and uncomfortable. He realised that he had been disturbed ever since that will of Laura Mildmay's had come into his office, more particularly since he had heard that the residuary legatee had quixotically insisted on following in her aunt's roving footsteps and coming to

New Zealand to collect her share.

As far as he knew everything was straightforward. The instructions under the will were clear. There could be no phoney business. Yet here was a blind-drunk housekeeper, a telephone with apparently no one at the other end ringing in the early hours of the morning, a girl slipping on wet seaweed. Seaweed, of all things!

Antonia said slowly, "I could have imagined all this, of course. I could have imagined that someone was in the house and that I heard the front door shut. I can swear the telephone rang, but that could have been a mistake, a wrong number. And I know I slipped" — she felt her forehead ruefully — "but the seaweed could have been left there from this morning. It would still be damp because this is a cold house, always full of draughts. And I suppose it's true that I could have imagined that scream, or screamed myself. The whole thing *is* explainable, as you can see."

She was giving the construction that other people, like Iris and Simon, would put on the affair. But all the time she was drawing his uneasy attention to the other side, the fact that someone, knowing Bella's weakness, might deliberately have put the slimy, slippery seaweed on the stairs and gone away and rung up at that improbable hour in the morning to lure Antonia downstairs.

That was the explanation Henrietta would gleefully seize on and elaborate. But even Henrietta's ingenious mind would not be able to name the culprit.

"Iris and Simon will be at Mount Cook by now," Dougal said, continuing his thoughts aloud.

"I know. Probably sound asleep."

"The air up there is very good," he said irrelevantly. "You should go there before you leave New Zealand. Then if by any chance there was any — any forethought given to this business—"

"You mean who did it? Oh, but I don't suppose anyone did. I expect Iris is quite right and I should see a doctor. You'll think so when I tell you what I'm thinking."

"What are you thinking?" he asked sharply.

"Of that man who rang me in Auckland. And who rang Iris yesterday. I know he did because I answered the phone. Iris was upset, too. And frightened. But she didn't say anything." Antonia's eyes went to the door. "I think he's not very far away."

"Come now! You'll believe in witches next," Dougal said explosively. "Whatever reason would an unknown man have for playing those tricks on you? You'd better get dressed and I'll take you home."

But she shook her head decisively.

"No, indeed. I'm not running away."

Dougal was exasperated.

"No one will say you are. But after the shock you've had you can't stay here alone."

"I'm not alone. Bella will wake up sometime, and there's Gussie. I've decided to try to improve Gussie's standard of education. I'm convinced it's just ignorance that makes him so difficult. I intend to give him lessons each morning."

Looking at her lying there with the bump on her forehead beginning to discolour, with shadows beneath her eyes and cheekbones prominent, Dougal was aware of his exasperation giving way to reluctant admiration. The girl was crazy, but she had spirit. Thinking of an unlikeable, sly, backward child after the sort of night through which she had been going.

"Gussie's education can be thought of later," he said. "If you won't come home with me I'll stay here with you."

Her eyes widened.

"Dougal! How sweet of you! When you don't even like me."

"Who said I didn't like you?" He was aware with annoyance of the colour rising in his cheeks.

"Well, we've been more or less fighting ever since we met. Personally I think you're sweet, but not just my type. And as for you, I can just visualise your kind of girl. Someone quiet, pretty and intelligent — oh, a very nice kind of girl."

Hearing his particular dream so accurately described made Dougal peculiarly angry.

"I suppose, to tell the truth, you just can't imagine anyone falling in love with me."

"Actually I can," she said gently. "Yes, indeed I can." She moved her swollen ankle slightly. "Even when I'm in this awful agony, I can!"

He made an exclamation of remorse.

"I'll get the stuff. I've left it on the stairs."

He was very expert in bathing and bandaging the ankle, and elevating it so that the pain would lessen. But it wasn't until they had shared the whisky remaining in Simon's last bottle that his apprehension began to lessen and Antonia began to chuckle.

"Query," she said, "does a drunken cook constitute a chaperone?"

She might have been killed tonight — by accident or design — yet she was laughing. She was refusing to be afraid. He had to pay tribute to her courage. He had to admire it.

# XI

It must have been that very liberal dose of whisky that Dougal had given her that made her sleep. It must have been the whisky, too, that had given her that queer dream that someone was crying, tiptoeing up and down the passage crying in smothered gasps.

Nothing could have been more normal now than the sunshine streaming through the open windows from a benignly blue sky. Antonia could hear Simon's birds twittering madly down in the hall, and dishes being rattled in the kitchen. She was conscious of a delicious lifting of her spirits that had nothing to do with the knowledge that the night was over or of the easing of the pain in her ankle.

She moved the bedclothes to look at her ankle, and seeing the neat bandage remembered Dougal's serious, absorbed face as he had wound it on. Then she remembered that in his discomfited way he had said he would stay until morning and she sat up, putting her foot experimentally out of bed.

As she did so Henrietta Conroy came in carrying a breakfast tray. She was beaming with pleasure and excitement, her mind eagerly lapping up the melodrama of the situation.

"My dear!" she said, "as soon as Dougal came in — and after daylight, too! — I knew something terrible had happened. Oh, I don't mean the sort of thing you're thinking. Poor Dougal, sometimes I think he's frightened of women, and no wonder, with a female like me about the place! No, I mean something really mysterious, like ropes across the stairs or poison in your coffee."

"But why?" Antonia asked reasonably.

"That's what we have to find out, love. When Dougal said you had slipped on the stairs and twisted your ankle" (Antonia could imagine his deliberately bald statement), "I said, 'There's more in this than meets the eye! I'm going right up there this minute.' So here I am, and I've got your breakfast because Bella looks a bit sick this morning. Says her stomach's bad. I couldn't be surprised if she had something malignant. She looks the colour, poor little scrap. And how is your ankle, dear?"

140

"It seems better, thank you."

"Don't put it to the ground yet." Henrietta's capable fingers felt the swelling gently. "Did Dougal put this bandage on?"

"Yes."

She chuckled. "He's practical, that's one thing." Then her sharp eyes, pregnant with anticipation, looked up at Antonia. "How did you come to slip, dear?"

"I was going to answer the telephone and there was a bit of seaweed—"

"A bit of what?"

"Seaweed. From the beach. I must have brought it in after I'd been swimming yesterday."

Henrietta dismissed that with her wide beaming smile.

"Now, love, don't be absurd! All that climb from the beach. As if any seaweed wouldn't have shaken off your clothes. No." She shook her head. "I'd say it was a deliberate plot."

With all the bright morning to reassure her Antonia smiled gaily.

"Who by, Henrietta?"

"Well, now, that's what we have to find out. My own son, as you will have discovered, has no imagination at all. He's completely prosaic. I suppose a solicitor has to be. All those whereas's and of the first parts. So we'll have to work

141

this out ourselves. Now first, who would want to murder you?"

Put baldly like that, it was a little disconcerting. If she gave all the knowledge she had to Henrietta, Henrietta in her light-hearted zestful hunger for excitement would turn it into something significant, frightening, horrible,... And it couldn't be! It couldn't be!

"Hasn't anyone a motive?" Henrietta probed.

Antonia forced herself to laugh.

"I wouldn't think so. Am I such a menace?"

Kindness filled Henrietta's broad plain face.

"No, indeed. And what am I doing talking to you about murder before you've had any breakfast. That's something that one shouldn't have to face on an empty stomach. Get yourself back to bed and have this nice hot coffee. Made by myself because I couldn't trust Bella. Oh. I don't mean she would do anything criminal, I mean that her mind doesn't seem to be functioning very well this morning. And listen, love, you're to come down to us until Iris and Simon return. It isn't safe for you here. Now quite honestly, quite apart from mysteries, it isn't safe for you to be here practically alone."

But there again Antonia had her curious stubborn determination to stay. It was more than that she would despise herself for cowardice if she went away. It was an intuition that something had to be discovered, someone had to be helped. She preferred to stay, she said flatly. Her ankle was a great deal better. She would be able to hobble about on a stick. There was nothing to be alarmed about. All that had happened was that she had had a fall.

It was difficult arguing with Henrietta who was deaf. Antonia finally convinced her of her intention, and Henrietta, after a long conference with Bella, left at last.

"Bella says her nerves are bad and she took something to make her sleep last night," she reported, as she was going. "That's why she didn't hear anything. But she's full of remorse and promises to sleep with one eye open tonight. I'm afraid I've frightened her a bit, but at least she won't neglect you. Promise to telephone the moment *anything* untoward happens, and do be careful to keep off that foot. Really, I think you're extraordinarily brave."

The way Henrietta looked at things, Antonia supposed she must seem very brave indeed. But with the sunlight and her own inner sense of happiness she felt there was no especial cause for bravery. She stayed in her room until after lunch which Bella, silent and shamefaced, brought to her, then she got the two sticks that Henrietta had thoughtfully left at her bedside and prepared to hobble downstairs.

As she reached the head of the stairs, however, the sound of voices made her pause. She peered over the banisters and saw Bella talking to two women who were just leaving. One, who seemed elderly and rather infirm, was clinging to the arm of the other. She had a flesh-coloured complexion and a vaguely distressed face. She seemed to be wiping tears from her eyes.

"I hope she won't fret any more now," Bella was saying in her quick sharp way. She was like a mouse talking, her thin beady-eyed face on one side, her voice issuing in thin light tones.

"No, you'll be all right, won't you, dear," the other woman answered, giving her companion a little reassuring shake. The elderly woman looked at Bella with a sad smile. Her voice, to Antonia, was almost inaudible.

"You can't bring them back when they're gone, can you?"

"That's the only way to look at it, dear," the other woman said briskly. "Come along now or we'll miss our tram. Your visit has done you good, hasn't it?"

"Oh, yes. I think so. I think so."

Something sad and lost about her voice made Antonia hobble back into her room to watch the two women go down the path, the stouter younger one supporting the drooping figure of the old one. There was something lonely about them, going out at the gate and down the hillside. The tussocks shone honey-gold in the sun, the road was white with dust. The slow black figures of the women were like shadows with nothing to cast them, shadows, defying the law of nature beneath the brilliant sun.

When she went downstairs there was an umbrella lying on the hall seat. It was a long, black, old-fashioned one, the sort old ladies carried on the finest days, and sometimes put up to shield them from the sun.

Antonia called to Bella.

"Your friends left an umbrella," she said.

Bella came hurrying into the hall. She had a startled look, almost as if she had been caught at something.

"What is it?"

"Just an umbrella. They won't get wet today."

"So it is. I'll hang it up. They'll call again I've no doubt."

"It's a steep climb up the hill for an old lady," Antonia observed. "I mean the little one."

"Yes, poor thing. She's lost her sister. Her niece thought a visit might do her good. Take her out of herself. She's an old friend of mine."

Antonia wondered if there was something worrying Bella. She was talking so quickly and

145

not looking directly at her. But of course —
she guessed Antonia knew about the empty
brandy bottle. Well, she was not going to be
the one to scold her. She began talking at ran-
dom to put Bella at her ease.

"My ankle feels much better. I'm not going
to be incapacitated for long after all. Wasn't it
silly, falling like that? Though I would like to
know who was ringing up at three o'clock in
the morning."

"I didn't hear a thing," Bella muttered.

(Of course you didn't. You were dead drunk.
Who gives you the brandy, Bella? You couldn't
afford to buy Courvoisier yourself.)

"The wind was making a lot of noise," Antonia said smoothly. (Were Bella's drunken
habits the reason she hadn't heard the crying
in the night, too?) "I must feed Simon's birds.
He'd be very angry if he knew they hadn't been
attended to yet. Then I want to see Gussie."

"Gussie?" Apprehension came into Bella's face.

"Yes. I thought that for as long as I'm here
I might do something about his education."
Her voice was earnest. "He's not getting a fair
chance, you know."

Bella's face lit up in the dim moving way it
had, like a candle in a very dark room. She
burst out, "Indeed, he's not. That's what I say.
He ought to have learning. Then he wouldn't

be bad. But I don't know enough to teach him, and he won't do the lessons the correspondence school sends."

"Do you think he'll listen to me?" Antonia asked.

"He might. Oh, Miss, if only you could help him."

Antonia patted the woman's thin shoulder. She had her troubles. One couldn't blame her for seeking comfort from a brandy bottle.

"You send him to me when he comes in."

"But, Miss—"

"Yes?"

"Will you be wanting to stay — I mean, after last night. Falling like that."

"Good gracious, I'm not going to let a fall frighten me. That was purely an accident. My feet are too big."

But she was aware of Bella's slanted eyes following her as she went out of the room. Bella, she realised, was disturbed by something, too. What was it? Would she be able to gain the frightened little woman's confidence?

She fed the birds, delighting in their quick neat movements, and their loving whispers into one another's ears. The lemon-coloured one, Simon's favourite, clung to the wires of the cage and talked to her in its intimate ghostly voice.

"Have a quick one! Have a quick one!"

Antonia smiled with pleasure. Simon had been trying to get the bird to say that and it stubbornly refused, confining itself to the simpler "Pretty boy". He would be delighted by this. It was almost worth ringing him up to tell him. Would Iris appreciate a message about Simon's birds on her honeymoon? Antonia thought not. Iris tolerated the birds, but she thought Simon's absorption in them a little childish. And she was possessive. Simon would have to be diplomatic about them.

It was as if her mind were divided into two compartments, one concerned only with the bright day, the chattering darting birds, the thought of attempting to improve Gussie's unwilling mind; the other shutting away the dark shadow of the night and its unexplained fears and apprehensions. She was a girl in a new country with a little money and a long life ahead of her. She was not going to let anything that happened at the Hilltop dismay or frighten her.

It was later in the afternoon that, passing Iris's room, she noticed the door wide open. It had been shut previously, she knew, and seeing it open made her pause to look in. It seemed to her that the bed was rumpled. She stepped into the room and saw at once the chaos on the dressing table, and the sprawling scarlet writing on the wall, the childish, "You are a wicked woman" scrawled in lipstick over the wallpaper, over Iris's expensive Regency striped wallpaper of which she had been so proud. Under the words were two initials. They looked like "L.M." but it seemed that the tail of the L was a mistake. The lipstick had slipped. The letter should have been an I. The message was intended to read, "You are a wicked woman, Iris Mildmay."

Whoever had written it had not only lain on the bed, rumpling the heavy gold covers, but had also had a wonderful time dabbling in Iris's cosmetics. The dressing table was covered in face powder, a lipstick lay on the floor, the room reeked of perfume. Antonia wrinkled her nose, identifying the expensive smell. Chanel of Lanvin, she thought. Iris wouldn't appreciate it being frivolously wasted. But that was nothing to the impudent message on the wall.

Antonia limped to the door.

"Bella," she called. "Bella."

Bella came so quickly, climbing the stairs with a sort of hopping gait, like a lame bird, that Antonia sensed that she too was on edge and nervously expectant. What *did* Bella know?

But when the little woman saw the room

with the disfigured wallpaper and the littered dressing table she gave a gasp of anger and despair.

"It's Gussie," she said. "That's his work. My, what I'll do to him. Just wait till I get him."

Half an hour ago Gussie had come back from the beach, dangling his fishing lines and whistling loudly. He wasn't far away now, and in a few minutes Bella came back, dragging him by one skinny wrist. He certainly was not a likeable child. He had the low brow of inferior intellect and a sharp sly long-chinned face. Now, scowling and sulky, he looked even less attractive.

His mother, out of breath, could scarcely get out her indignant accusation.

"Look at that, you bad boy! Whatever made you do a terrible thing like that?"

Gussie's sly eyes went over the scrawling writing.

"Gosh!" he murmured, as if in awed admiration for someone's superior nerve. One wouldn't have guessed he had the ability to act, but a boy of his nature would be full of cunning.

"Don't say 'gosh' like that! What made you do it? You little devil!"

Bella took him by his lank forelock and shook him violently. He gave a screech of protest.

"But I didn't do it! Honest, I didn't!"

"You needn't make it worse by lying. Who else would do it, tell me that? Who else would play a trick like that?"

"But I never came in here. I've never been in this bloody room before."

It almost seemed his protestations had a ring of truth. If they had Bella didn't hear it. Or she pretended not to. Was there fear in her eyes? If there was it would be fear for what Iris would say when she returned.

"And don't you use that bad language," she went on. "Look at that scent spilt. Costs a fortune, it does. Smell it."

Gussie turned up his nose defiantly.

"It stinks," he said.

"Stinks or not, what made you *do* it?"

"But I didn't, Ma. I didn't."

Antonia had a queer feeling that she was watching a drama enacted for her benefit. Someone had disfigured Iris's room and willy nilly Gussie had to be the culprit. But was he? If he were not it was utterly unfair to punish him.

"If that's your writing, Gussie," she said, "it's shocking. You've certainly got to start doing some work. Suppose we start right away. Bella, I think it might be a good idea to lock this door while Mrs. Mildmay is away. I'll try to find out in town the best thing to remove lipstick."

151

Bella looked her gratitude. Gussie merely scowled. He scowled harder than ever when Antonia sat him at a table with a sheet of paper and a pencil and set him to writing all the letters of the alphabet.

"You can't make me do this if I don't want to," he scoffed.

"I don't suppose I can," Antonia answered. With his low brow, his narrow eyes and his sulky mouth Gussie really was quite the most unlikeable child she had ever met. But someone ought to persevere with him. "And let me tell you it doesn't matter in the least to me if you can never write a line. But some day you may want to sign a cheque or write a letter to your girl, and then you'll be sorry if you can't make a respectable job of it."

"Nuts!" said Gussie. He began to stick the point of the pencil through the paper. Then he boasted, "Some day I'll write a cheque for a fousand pounds. A fousand pounds."

"Well, let's practise now," Antonia suggested reasonably. She wrote in large letters 'Pay to Antonia Webb the sum of One thousand pounds'. How funny it would be to have a sum of money on which to draw cheques. But it was really more fun having none, and always working hard for something, a new dress or a set of golf clubs or a holiday, savouring one's prize to the utmost, like someone with an appetite whetted by abstinence. The flavour of life came from anticipation, not realisation.

"I know something you don't know," said Gussie, laboriously making a large A.

"What's that?"

"Something no one else knows."

"Yes?" Antonia betrayed no interest. The child was contrary enough to close his tight mouth and say nothing more if she appeared too eager to know what it was that cried in the night or who put seaweed on the stairs.

"Will Miss Matthews think it was me who wrote with the lipstick?"

"I'm afraid so."

"I don't care. I hate her."

"That's not the way to write an A. Look, like this. What were you going to tell me that you knew?"

"Something she gave me. I've hidden it."

"Gussie!" That was Bella's voice sharply from the doorway. "Attend to your work and don't talk. Don't listen to him, Miss. He makes things up."

Gussie put his tongue out at his mother. Then he closed his narrow unchildish mouth and not another sound came from it. The curious thing, Antonia noticed, was that his awkward babyish handwriting bore little resemblance

to that on the wall in Iris's room. He could perhaps have had the cunning to disguise it. She
didn't think such an illiterate child would have
that ability.

That evening Iris telephoned from the Hermitage at Mount Cook where she and Simon were
spending their brief honeymoon. The telephone bell sent Antonia's heart fluttering now.
Each time she lifted the receiver she expected
to hear the voice of the unknown man who
mysteriously knew much more about them
than they did about him. (She still refused to
believe Iris's explanation that he was merely
someone looking for accommodation.)

When she lifted the receiver, however, it was
Iris's voice that came lilting over the wire.

"Hullo, Tonia. How are you now?" Her
voice was full of sympathy and concern.

"I'm perfectly all right, thank you," Antonia
answered in some surprise. "Why do you ask?"

"I've just had to ring Dougal Conroy about
a business matter and he told me about last
night. Darling, I'm so concerned. Really, you
mustn't stay alone any longer."

So Iris was back on the sleep-walking or the
amnesia theory.

"There's no need whatever to be concerned
about me," Antonia said rather coldly. It was
no use trying to explain anything to Iris. She

154

wouldn't believe anything, not even the ringing of the telephone. She would say, "Poor Antonia. She must see a doctor about her nerves." Was she being genuinely kind or deliberately blind?

"Please darling," she went on. "Stay with the Conroys at night. Henrietta tells me she is urging you to. Simon and I are coming back on Tuesday."

"Are you having a nice time?" Antonia asked politely.

"Oh, perfectly wonderful! I admit I don't care for the mountains, they make me feel so *small!* But we've met some lovely people. That's why I'm ringing you — we're bringing some people back with us. They want to be in Christchurch for the flower festival next week-end, and they just can't get accommodation. So with the big house what could I do? I wonder, darling, if you could arrange to have two rooms ready. A double one and a single one. I didn't mean to have anyone until the alterations were done, but these people beg to come. They're a Mr. and Mrs. Halstead and a Doctor Bealey. You'll like Doctor Bealey. He's so dark and distinguished. They say they won't mind roughing it. Two of the best rooms in the empty wing, darling. But don't run about on your bad ankle. Do everything by telephone. And *do* be diplomatic with Bella. She's a gem if you treat her right. Henrietta says she'll send Ethel up to help. And Henrietta will help you about where to order provisions. And drinks, darling. Could you remember to have some brandy and gin and bitters, and whisky, too, if you can get it. I'm arranging for the builders to start next week, too. But I'll do that when I get back. It's going to be *fun!*"

There was an excited breathlessness about all this that left Antonia a little out of breath herself. Iris sounded as if she were suffering from some powerful excitement. Surely being married to quiet old Simon wasn't having this effect on her.

"I'll do my best," she promised. It would be reassuring having other people in the house, to fill the rooms with their chatter and to check on any mysterious noises or events.

"I knew you would," Iris said gratefully in her high excited voice. "It's wonderful to have you there. But are you *sure* you're all right after that fall? That nasty bump on your head, too."

"My head's perfectly all right."

"Thank goodness for that. *Do* be careful. *Do* promise to stay with the Conroys until we get back. Oh, here's Simon wanting to talk to you."

The next moment Simon's slow voice sounded in her ear.

"Hullo, Antonia. Sorry you had that accident. How are the birds?"

"Very well, Simon."

"Johnnie?"

"Oh, he'll surprise you. He's learnt a new sentence."

"*No!*" Simon's voice was full of surprised delight. "What is it?"

"Have a quick one."

"No! The little rascal! Well, I say!" Simon was chuckling with pleasure. "The moment my back's turned. I say, Iris, Johnnie is saying, 'Have a quick one.' Sorry, Antonia, I was telling Iris. She says that we ought to be taking Johnnie's advice right now."

"Are you happy, Simon?" Antonia asked lightly.

"Happy! I just can't believe it." Simon's voice sounded bewildered. "Truly, I just can't believe it."

The funny thing, Antonia reflected as she hung the receiver up, was that she felt Simon's happiness was not quite genuine. He was dazzled, he was in transports, but he was bewildered, too. Iris's quick sophisticated mind was always going to perplex him and leave him behind. She was not going to be an easy wife. Already he was turning to his birds for rest and peace.

# XII

At the office on Monday morning Miss Fox, as usual, intercepted Dougal.

"Good morning, Mr. Conroy," she said with her everlasting brightness.

"Good morning, Miss Fox," Dougal had alternated all the weekend between affability and dejection, both inexplicable. He hadn't gone fishing after all, but he might as well have got away, for Antonia had stubbornly refused to leave the Hilltop, except during the daytime when she had long consultations with Henrietta on the preparations to be made for the expected guests. He had been pushed aside as being of little value in this kind of crisis, and he had moodily watched Ethel bustling about getting ready to go up to the Hilltop, and giggling immoderately as Henrietta called instructions.

Henrietta had never been so much in her element. At one moment she was predicting Antonia's death by murder or manslaughter, and the next she was saying that she had known all along that Iris would never spend one week at the Hilltop without filling the place with people. She would want plenty of gaiety. She would be leading a wild life up there. Simon as a husband was only a blind. She shouted gossip in her penetrating voice and turned her wholly charming smile on everyone. She was enjoying herself tremendously. Drama had come into her life at last, if only vicariously.

But Dougal had been glad when the weekend was over. He found Antonia's presence a curious irritation and her absence a great anxiety. It was a relief to get back to Miss Fox's bright impersonal stare.

"Anything special in the mail, Miss Fox?"

"Just this letter from Mr. Mildmay confirming Mrs. Mildmay's telephone request for another advance."

"Yes, that will be right," Dougal said.

"That will be two thousand pounds they've had now," Miss Fox pointed out.

"I know. It's perfectly all right. We'll arrange for probate to be produced to the bank and then we can draw on the estate account."

"Why are they in such a hurry for another

five hundred pounds?" Miss Fox inquired.

"The first advance was made to enable them to buy the Hilltop, as you know, and now they want to start on the alterations sooner than they had intended doing. That's all. Is anything wrong?"

"No. Except that most builders don't require to be paid in advance."

That thought had occurred to Dougal, too. But that was Simon's business. He might not have cared to admit that Iris was already fleecing him, or he might not have known. He might have thought the money genuinely was required for the builders. For that matter, probably it was. Five hundred pounds was too much to require for a private reason. Anyway, so long as the matter was legally in order it was no business of either his or Miss Fox's.

"Have a cheque ready for them tomorrow," Dougal said briskly, ignoring Miss Fox's comment. "Is there anything else?"

"The Coldharbour transfer is ready to be settled. Miss Perkins wants to add a codicil to her will. Mr. Dunlop wants you to ring him about that City Council lease. By the way, there was something else about the Mildmays."

Dougal couldn't help looking up sharply. The Mildmays were absorbing too much of his time and interest.

"Yes?"

"Well, you know after we got that letter last week we thought we'd check on the *Canton's* passenger list."

"Yes."

"I did that at the shipping office, but there was no Iris Matthews on the passenger list for that particular trip."

"You mean the trip Laura Mildmay was on?"

"Yes, that one."

Dougal looked at Miss Fox. He could see that she was bursting to tell him something else, that she had carefully repressed the desire ever since he had come into the office.

"Well?" he said.

"There were two elderly people on that trip who live in Christchurch. I recognised their names. I took the liberty of ringing them up."

Dougal narrowed his eyes.

"Was that discreet?"

Miss Fox looked pained.

"I don't know. *I* tried to be. I said I was trying to trace a friend who I thought had come out on the *Canton*. I described her."

"And did they recognise her?" Dougal couldn't help but be interested. He felt that Miss Fox was as prying as his mother, but somehow that her curiosity was justified.

"Not as a passenger," Miss Fox answered primly. Her eyes glinted behind her thick glasses. "They said that the only person who answered to that description was one of the stewardesses. But of course it was most unlikely that my friend would have been a stewardess."

"Did the name correspond?" Dougal asked sharply.

"No, it didn't. This stewardess was a Mrs. Cox. But that doesn't necessarily mean a thing. She could have used another name if she didn't want her friends to know what she was doing."

Who were Iris's friends? Unfortunately, whoever they were they were not in New Zealand. Iris was clever and quick and sophisticated, but she could also be a good actress. Had she graduated from a servant or had she come upon bad times? Either was possible. If she were a servant she might have looked on Simon's ten thousand pounds as a fortune and married him for it. On the whole, that seemed the most likely explanation. One way or another it didn't seem very important except as far as Simon was concerned, and he was old enough to look after himself.

Dougal went into his office and sat down.

"All right, Miss Fox. Bring your book in and we'll draft that lease."

Miss Fox looked disappointed. She had enjoyed her small sleuthing job, obviously.

Equally obviously, she was not enamoured of the new Mrs. Mildmay.

"That information about Mrs. Mildmay can be pigeon-holed," he said. "We may need to check on it further sometime. But I shouldn't think so."

"Yes, Mr. Conroy." Miss Fox dismissed the subject as he had wanted her to. She produced her shorthand book and settled herself neatly. "Did you have a good fishing this weekend, Mr. Conroy?"

"I didn't go upcountry this weekend."

"Oh, what a pity!"

She was inquisitive again, peering at him beneath her glasses. The devil take these women! Couldn't he have any privacy? Were they going to ferret out his uneasy unwilling interest in a red-headed girl this early? It was bad enough having it keep him awake himself. But it was his own problem and it would remain so.

# XIII

Late on Tuesday afternoon Iris and Simon arrived home. Iris came in carrying a large wicker basket. She set it down carefully on a chair in the hall and went to kiss Antonia. Her skin was wind-burnt, her nose peeling. Against the unaccustomed colour in her skin her eyes were like green water.

"Darling, you're still all right," she cried. "Thank God for that. No more falls? No more frights?" Her eyes were anxious and concerned.

"None at all," said Antonia lightly.

"And your ankle?"

"It's all right as long as I don't walk on it too much. Where's Simon? What's in the basket?"

"Simon's struggling with the luggage. He's so slow! What's in the basket? Ah, but you wait and see. Shut all the doors, will you, please."

Antonia obeyed in some perplexity. Iris lifted the lid of the basket, and out stepped a magnificent white Persian cat. With great composure it strolled round the hall, investigating its whereabouts.

"Isn't he beautiful?" Iris whispered. "One of the guides at the Hermitage gave him to me, or rather I practically cajoled him away. I paid for him, of course. Probably far more than Ptolemy is worth. The guide's wife had died and there was no one to look after Ptolemy when he was away on expeditions. Simon, I might tell you, wasn't very keen, but after all he has his birds."

At that moment the front door opened and Simon, carrying the bags, came in. Almost in the same instant Ptolemy saw the bird cage and made a powerful spring, coming up against the wire with a clatter that sent all the birds fluttering and screeching.

Simon dropped the bags and made a rush forward, his face scarlet with apprehension.

"Iris! I told you what would happen! He'll frighten them to death."

Iris, too, sprang forward to clutch the cat and fondle him in her arms. He struggled and showed his claws, the pupils of his eyes blacking out the green. Above him, Iris's eyes, the same green, were bland and a little amused.

"Now, darling, don't get upset. He can't get

your precious birds. He'll soon learn to leave them alone."

"No he won't. A cat goes on stalking."

"Well, and if he does he can't get at them." Iris began to pout. "Surely I'm to be allowed a pet when you have all those."

The birds' screeching died down and Simon's face became contrite.

"Of course you are. I'm sorry. That was mean of me. I guess we can make sure Ptolemy can't get through the wires. There you are, Antonia. I haven't even got round to saying hullo to you. I say, that's a nasty bruise you've still got."

Simon's change from anger to anxious placation was curiously disturbing. If Iris got too domineering he would lose all his spirit. It almost seemed as if she had procured this cat out of jealousy of Simon's birds.

"Yes, isn't it," said Iris. "Antonia, you must tell us exactly what happened that night."

"Later," Antonia said. "First, Bella has tea ready, and then I'm afraid we have to tell you about an unfortunate episode. Bella blames Gussie for it, but he denies it."

"He would. It will be him, of course. The little horror! What has he done now?"

"He's made rather a mess with your lipstick. We've tried to take it off, but the paper hangers say the only thing is to paper over it."

"Where?" Iris demanded. "Not in my room?"

It was unfortunate that they hadn't been able to erase the words. The spiteful message across Iris's wall was quite plain. As Iris read it her mouth tightened and she went rather white. Simon beside her slipped his hand through her arm.

"The little hound. I'll whip him."

To Antonia's surprise, Iris shook her head. She spoke a little breathlessly, as if a boy's mischief had made her more frightened than angry.

"No. I'll see Bella. Gussie's just ignorant. Anyway, I guess it was my fault for leaving lipstick about. Thanks, Tonia, for doing what you could. And now what about the other rooms? Joyce and David Halstead are arriving tomorrow morning, and Doctor Bealey in the afternoon."

Antonia told them what had been done, and Iris became absorbed in her plans. It seemed as if she were determined to make little account of Gussie and his rude message. She had come back filled with energy and goodwill. Her little pointed face sparkled. If she had never been still before now she moved about twice as restlessly. All the time her eyes held a look of intense excitement.

The first night she was loving to Simon, kind to Bella and Gussie, and full of enthusiasm

167

for Antonia's efforts in preparing two bedrooms in the empty wing. She got out furniture catalogues and planned colour schemes, and discussed extra staff, waitresses, maids, and gardeners. Simon looked bewildered but quite amenable and content. This was Iris's show and she was bound to make a success of it. As long as it made her happy she could turn the place inside out. But he was tired from travelling all day and wanted to go to bed early. Perhaps, too, he was eager to share the wide bed in Iris's room and not trudge down to the hotel in Sumner. It was the new regime, Antonia thought, not entirely with amusement, for it disturbed her to think of Simon lying in the big bed reading the splotched red writing on the wall, "You are a wicked woman!" and knowing that it referred to his wife.

After he had gone upstairs Iris picked up the white cat and wandered about in her long green housecoat, her sharp chin tucked into the cat's fur. She seemed reluctant to follow Simon. She was too restless. When Antonia, too, rose to go it seemed as if the excitement in her eyes turned to apprehension. For a moment she had a look of silently begging Antonia not to leave her alone.

But that must have been Antonia's imagination, for she said lightly, "Have a good night.

No sleep-walking now." She rubbed her wind-burnt nose. "I must do something about this atrocity if I can keep my eyes open long enough. Simon sleeps like a *log.*"

In spite of her professed tiredness, however, Antonia heard Iris walking about on her slip-pered feet long after she herself was in bed. Was it Simon who slept like a log in her bed that kept her up, or was she too excited, too apprehensive of something, to sleep?

The Halsteads arrived in the morning. They were a nice enough couple, quite undistin-guished, he with a round unintelligent good-humoured face and she loud-voiced, talkative, and inclined to laugh a lot. She had a very new permanent wave, the tight curls emphasising the lines in her face, and her clothes lacked imagination, to say the least. Antonia was a little mystified as to why Iris had exerted her-self for such ordinary people.

It was a warm day, and after lunch Iris sug-gested that they all go down to the beach for a swim. Antonia, because her ankle still pained her and she didn't think she could manage the steep path down the cliff, excused herself. Inevitably Iris fussed, and insisted on her lying on the couch in the lounge with her foot up for the afternoon. She drew the blinds so that only chinks of sunlight came in, and in yellow gloom her fair face floated like an inverted flower.

"You have a sleep, dear. The house will be absolutely quiet. We won't be back until the sun has gone."

The house was so alive with sleepy sounds, the ticking of a clock, the muted chattering of Simon's birds, the gentle hushing of the wind and the distant crash of the sea on the rocks that Antonia did fall asleep. She thought she was on a little boat, dipping up and down on the sparkling waves, the sun as warm as firelight on her face. She stirred because a chink of sunlight through the venetian blinds did in reality lie across her eyes, and at the same moment she was aware of the face bending over her.

A narrow pale face curiously disembodied.

She was still half in her dream, and the face, shadowy in the gloom, seemed full of menace. She thought she heard a voice murmuring with a gloating sound, "Don't be afraid, my dear. It'll soon be over."

Opening her eyes wide she scrambled up, drawing herself back on the couch.

The man's form moved.

"Don't be afraid." He really was speaking and he really was saying those identical words. But they had no menacing quality now. They were polite and apologetic. "Did I startle you?

I thought you were Mrs. Mildmay. I shouldn't have barged in like this, but the door was open. There seems to be no one else home."

"They're all down at the beach," Antonia said breathlessly. Then she was instantly sorry she had made that admission. For although now she was fully awake the queer sense of danger persisted. She had an overwhelming desire to get out of the room quickly. But one couldn't do that. It was absurd.

She limped to the windows to pull up the blinds. The sunlight flooded in, and with the reassurance that gave her she said, "You must be Doctor Bealey. I remember now. Iris said she was expecting you this afternoon."

"That's right," said the man, and Antonia turned from the windows to look at him, her equanimity recovered.

Then she had her second shock. For the youngish man with a slightly crooked thin nose, the close-set dark eyes and the yellowish pallor was the man who had stared at her so persistently in the plane the other day. How did he come to be here at the Hilltop? Surely it was not by accident. Surely it was by design.

"And you're Miss Webb," he was saying easily.

"How do you know that?" Her voice was sharp with suspicion.

"Why, Iris told me about you, of course."

Of course that would be how it was. Doctor Bealey couldn't have deliberately spied on her and followed her here.

"I noticed you were limping," he was saying. "Have you hurt yourself?"

"Just a sprained ankle."

"A fall?" Was his voice more than politely interested? Was there that gloating note in it?

Before she could answer, however, footsteps clattered in the hall. Iris came hurrying in crying, "Oh, Ralph! I didn't think you would be here until this evening. What a good thing someone was here to welcome you. I see you and Antonia have made yourselves acquainted."

"Oh, but we'd met before today," Antonia said levelly.

Iris flashed her a startled glance. Ralph Bealey gave a small smile. His lips were a straight line, neither turning up nor down when he smiled.

"Ah, in the plane the other day. Is that what you're referring to, Miss Webb? But one could hardly have called that a meeting, much as I would like it to have been one. I'm flattered that you remembered me."

(He's talking like a book, Antonia thought, as if he's studied his part. Who and what is he?)

"But how extraordinary!" Iris was exclaiming. "What a coincidence. Well, there you are, Ralph, I told you Antonia was an attractive girl."

"Surely you didn't advertise me as part of your cuisine," Antonia said lightly.

"No, indeed! I tried to discourage him from coming. But accommodation in town is impossible this week, with the flower festival on. I'm afraid you'll have to rough it here, Ralph."

The man's dark eyes rested on Antonia. As in the plane his gaze made her feel acutely uncomfortable. She couldn't connect him with anything that had happened, his voice didn't remotely resemble the one on the telephone, yet his presence persisted in giving her this odd feeling of danger.

"I'll sleep on straw, if need be," he said. "Ah, there's Simon. Hullo, old man. I've arrived, as you see."

"As I see," Simon repeated. He had on an old grey jersey and a pair of shapeless flannel trousers. His mouth was open a little. He looked quite stupid.

Iris gave him an impatient nudge.

"Simon! You look as if you've had too much sun. Take the bags up and show Ralph his room."

"Oh, yes! Oh, yes!" Now Simon was offensively hearty. "Mine host, you see. Follow me, doctor. And don't mind the bare boards. We're

173

not ready for guests yet. You've gate-crashed."

Ralph Bealey went out with him and Iris turned to Antonia. Her face was narrowed and angry.

"If Simon's going to behave like that how *can* I run an hotel?"

"He sounded as if he didn't much care for Doctor Bealey," Antonia observed.

"And that's just childishness because Ralph monopolised a little, just a *little* of my time at the Hermitage. Really. Simon can't go through life being that jealous."

Then Iris's face cleared. "But now he'll see how silly he is because obviously it's you Ralph likes. And he never said a word about seeing you on the plane."

"Well, he wouldn't be expecting to find me here," Antonia said practically.

"Ah, yes, he would. If he were interested in a girl he'd find out who she was and where she lived, you can rely on that. He's a shrewd one."

"Why, who is he? Have you known him before?"

"I met him in Auckland at a party. So of course we recognised one another when we met at the Hermitage. He's come down here to start a practice in Christchurch." Her eyes gleamed suddenly. "We might get him to look you over while he's here."

In a vivid flash her queer meeting with the man came back to her, the strangely menacing pale face floating over her in the warm drowsy gloom. Her impressions had been distorted by sleep, they must be false, yet she knew she would never forget them.

"No, thank you," she said definitely.

"Why not? You aren't very well, you know. And Ralph's a little of a psychiatrist, too."

"No!" said Antonia firmly. "I don't need any doctor."

"All right, darling. It was only a suggestion. Actually, I think you are looking better. And we're going to be much gayer here now. Supposing we begin by having a little celebration tonight. We've got all that gin and stuff. I'm sure Henrietta and Dougal would come up. It would be fun."

Much as Antonia would have like it to be fun, and much as she tried to seem light-hearted, she couldn't enjoy the dances Ralph Bealey requested of her. The tables in the dining-room had been pushed to one side and they were dancing to a gramophone. Iris moved dreamily in David Halstead's arms, and Henrietta Conroy danced energetically with Simon, talking all the time in her penetrating voice. Dougal, with a curiously set expression on his face, guided another chatterer in Joyce Halstead, and Bella, assisted by Gussie, changed the records on the gramophone. It seemed as if Ralph Bealey's long cold hands were on her back and her arm all the time. His black hair receded in a thinning line on his high pale forehead and dark bristle showed through the pallor of his chin.

Some people would think him good looking. She couldn't explain the peculiar aversion she had for him. Probably it was quite unfair and unjustified. She ought to get to know him better before she decided so thoroughly that she disliked him.

Simon, as barkeeper, was lavish with the drinks, and gradually the evening blurred a little. Ralph Bealey's face was white and black, Simon's red, Dougal Conroy's faintly golden. The other night she had wanted Dougal to kiss her. Now he was far off, always in that silly noisy Joyce Halstead's or Iris's arms. Bella was having drinks, too, and by mistake putting on an occasional minuet or nocturne instead of a two-step.

Antonia escaped from Ralph Bealey and went over to Simon. He thought she wanted to dance and held out his arms.

"Simon, where does Bella get her brandy from?" she asked.

His little bright eyes between their puffy

lids looked at her in alarm.

"Brandy?"

"Yes. Dougal and I found her the other night dead drunk."

Simon gave an embarrassed, "Tch! Tch! She must buy it."

"Don't be absurd! How could she afford to? Does she pinch it?"

"Well—" His eyes slid away. "As a matter of fact — mind you, I don't approve. I've told Iris I don't approve. But it's damned hard getting a woman to stay up here. And if we put up with that awful young rascal of a son of hers I guess a bottle or so here and there—" His voice trailed away. Antonia thought, "The first night I was to spend here alone she had one. Was there any significance in that? No, of course not. It would be to celebrate their wedding. Simon would be feeling generous."

But the feeling persisted that it might be convenient for them that Bella drank. Sometimes it might be convenient. Such as when someone or something cried in the night. . . .

"Simon, I found a long grey hair in one of the empty rooms."

Simon stared at her with what seemed to be complete amazement.

"What on earth made you pick that up? How disgusting!" Then he said, "We had a char in once or twice. What a funny girl you are."

A charwoman. That would be the explanation, of course. Simon was right. She was being foolish.

Simon, dancing a little unsteadily, was now pursuing his own thoughts.

"I wish Iris hadn't wanted that cat. It's unfair of me not to let her have a pet, but I'm nervous about my birds. If he should get one he'd tear it to bits in a minute. Tear it to bits."

"Antonia!" came Dougal's voice. "It's time you danced with me." He had her in his arms almost before Simon had vaguely relinquished her. In the first step he trod on her toe.

"Oh, how clumsy you are!" she exclaimed exaggeratedly.

"Sorry! I know that other fellow's a better dancer than me."

"You mean Doctor Bealey? Yes, he dances very well." Perversity made her refrain from adding that she would prefer to dance with anyone in the world rather than Doctor Bealey.

"You shouldn't be dancing on that ankle, anyway," he said disapprovingly.

"I know. It's beginning to swell. Isn't it odd, Dougal, Ralph Bealey was that man I told you about in the plane."

Now she had his startled interest. His clear blue eyes, wide apart beneath their thick golden brows, stared at her. She looked back into them, taking deep pleasure in their straightness, their lack of guile.

"He wanted to meet me," she said dreamily.

"That old stuff!" There was contempt in his voice.

"It still works. At least Ralph thinks it does."

"And do you?"

She smiled. She wanted to feel the kitten's tongue roughness of his skin against her cheek again. She wanted to listen to him talking, just about anything at all. She mustn't have any more gin or she would begin to think she was in love with this nice, honest, unimaginative New Zealand solicitor. It was unlikely he would return her love and then she would be extremely unhappy. It was safer not to be in love.

"Me! Oh, anything works if you like a person."

His face stiffened. He trod on her toe again and said angrily, "Sorry! Are you sure he's not a fortune hunter?"

Antonia laughed merrily.

"Dougal! this is 1951. Four thousand pounds isn't even remotely a fortune. It's only some people's income tax."

"Are you sure—" Dougal was beginning, when suddenly there was a loud screeching and spitting from the hall. Iris darted to the door.

"Gussie!" she screamed. "Gussie, put that cat down!"

Gussie, Antonia saw, as she too reached the door, had Ptolemy held firmly by his four paws, two in each hand. He was swinging him in a circle while the cat struggled and spat. As Iris ran forward Gussie retreated to the stairway.

"See!" he cried in wicked glee. "See him doing a nose dive."

He swung the frenzied animal in another wild swoop, then with a last screech Ptolemy escaped him and fled for the open door.

Iris, beside herself with rage, reached Gussie and slapped him stingingly on either cheek.

"You little brute! You heartless little brute!"

"*Ah!*" gasped Bella in pain.

Gussie rubbed his cheek. He began to whimper.

"I'll tell on you. I'll tell something you don't want me to."

Bella ran unsteadily forward.

"Gussie, come here! Can't you keep out of mischief, you little devil!"

Iris turned her flushed angry face.

"Bella, for goodness' sake keep him under control. He's getting impossible. First that

180

mess in my room, and now this."

Bella put her arm round the boy roughly but not unkindly. Gussie had his arm crooked over his eyes.

"Her hit me!" he muttered. "I'll tell Miss Webb what—"

"You be quiet now," Bella hissed. "You come and get off to bed."

"Yes, take him to bed, Bella." Suddenly Iris sounded very tired. She gave a brilliant but worn smile at her guests. "Sorry for that diversion, folks. Gussie, as you will perceive, is something of a problem child."

Simon went to take her hand, in a kind of clumsy embarrassment, as if he couldn't get used to fondling her in public.

"Don't let it worry you, sweet. If Gussie's going to be too troublesome—"

But Iris had resolutely recovered her self-control. She said remorsefully, "No, we must be more patient with him. Poor little devil, he hasn't had a chance. And Ptolemy wasn't hurt. I don't think Gussie would really hurt him. I shouldn't have lost my temper. Let's all have another drink."

The scene, however, had spoilt the party, and it broke up within a few minutes. The Conroys went home and the Halsteads and Doctor Bealey to the bed in the other wing.

Antonia, vaguely distressed that in the general upset Dougal hadn't had an opportunity to say good night to her alone (would he have wanted to?) went slowly upstairs to her room. She didn't feel even remotely sleepy. She stood for a while at the open window watching the lights twinkling over the bay and listening to the dull thunder of the sea on the rocks below. The wind was almost still tonight. There was no sound of the melancholy whistling buoy. It was a good night for the first night Iris's guests spent here. They would at least be able to sleep soundly.

(If it had been seagulls that had cried that first night why had she never heard them again?)

Presently, down the hillside, she distinguished the light going on in the Conroy house and she thought with affection of Henrietta's big generous face and wild theories. His mother's colourful mind and interminable chatter would tend to make Dougal reserved. What went on in his mind? Why did he look at her with that slight frown of perplexity as if something about her was worrying him? Why, after all the men she had met, did this quiet-eyed, golden-browed young man in New Zealand have to get so frequently into her thoughts?

Antonia heard Simon's heavy footsteps down

the passage. She heard him yawn loudly and start making bumping movements in the bedroom. Then abruptly something slithered in the passage. Iris's voice came in a loud angry whisper, "Get downstairs, you bad boy! At once."

Antonia went to the door to see Iris clutching Gussie's thin shoulder and pushing him to the staircase.

"What's he doing up here?" she called.

Iris turned a flushed face.

"Heaven knows! I'm just about tired of him." She gave Gussie a final push. "Now get away downstairs to bed."

She came along to Antonia's room.

"What a child! Can I come in and have a cigarette?" She was breathing quickly and her eyes were too bright again.

"Yes, do. I'm wide awake myself. Gussie is getting naughty, isn't he?"

"Oh, he's impossible. It's only because I'm sorry for his mother that I tolerate him at all. Now he's getting a new trick of making up the most extraordinary stories. Tell me, has he been running to you with any of them?"

"He said he was going to tell me about something someone gave him. That's all. I didn't pay much attention."

Antonia lit a cigarette and watched Iris. She

walked to the window and drew the curtains across in a quick movement.

"I wonder what it was. But children of that age attach so much importance to nothing at all." She sat down and inhaled smoke, sighing deeply. "God, I'm tired now. Wasn't it a nice party until Gussie spoilt it? Tell me, did you like Ralph Bealey?"

"He dances well," Antonia said non-committally.

"I know. And his manners are entrancing. I think he's rather a pet. He'll definitely be our medical adviser. He has taken rooms in town, you know, but so far he hasn't found a place to live. He'll marry, of course."

"I daresay he will," Antonia murmured. What was in Iris's devious mind now?

"As a matter of fact," she went on honestly, "I didn't quite trust him."

Iris opened her eyes wide.

"Not trust him! Whatever do you mean? Surely you aren't old-fashioned to think he's going to seduce you!"

"It wasn't seduction I was thinking of," Antonia answered coolly.

"Then what are you thinking of?"

"I don't really know. I should think he's a very devious person."

"Darling, you shouldn't always analyse people like that. Accept them, enjoy them as I do. I think Ralph's quite charming, and if you only knew it your prejudice simply arises from this peculiar antagonism you have for doctors. It's a psychosis you have. But let's not worry about it now. I'll leave you to get a good sleep. Good night, dear." She bent to put her cool lips against Antonia's forehead. "You must rest more. Don't get up until late in the morning."

In bed Antonia fell asleep almost at once, but she had a disturbing dream about Ralph Bealey in which his hands, enlarged to gigantic proportions, were twice the size of his body, and he was coming towards her with the fingers curled. Then, as she frantically pushed them away she found she was holding a telephone and a low whispering voice was saying, "It's your turn next. It's your turn next."

And then the scream came.

That wasn't part of her dream. She was positive it wasn't. She sat upright, her heart pounding, perspiration cold on her forehead.

Now there was no sound at all except the sighing of the pines, and the faint intermittent clatter of the flax bush. She forced herself to get out of bed and go to the window.

Moonlight lay over the hillside, and sparkled in a cold colourless light on the water. The only movement in the garden was the slight bowing of tree shadows. There were no lights on in the house. No one else had been disturbed. *Had* she heard that scream?

Doubtful now, she was just going back to bed when she heard stealthy footsteps up the stairs. A chink of light showed under her door and then moved away.

All her impulse was to dive into bed and hide trembling beneath the blankets. But that way she would never find out anything. With a superhuman effort she made herself cross to the door and throw it open.

Someone a little way down the passage turned sharply, and a flashlight went out.

"Oh, is that you, Tonia?" Iris whispered. She was out of breath and breathing in great gulps. "Did I disturb you? I went down for Ptolemy. He was fighting with a great tomcat. I heard him screech."

In the darkness Antonia could just distinguish the pale blur of the cat against Iris's breast. She gave a deep sigh of relief.

"I heard that screech, too. I thought it was someone screaming."

"And no wonder." Iris was beginning to recover her breath. "He has a voice like a banshee. Haven't you, sweetie? I'm sorry you were disturbed, Antonia. Go back to bed and get some sleep."

# XIV

His slapping the previous evening had done Gussie good for he had got up early and cleaned all the shoes. But Iris had to confess that his good intentions had broken down at that stage and he had sneaked off fishing before breakfast.

"One can be too lenient with a boy of that type," Doctor Bealey observed. "The only thing they really respect is severity, and Gussie obviously doesn't get that from his mother."

"Well, we'll know in future," said Iris. "Tell me, did everyone sleep well? I did, when I had settled a fight between Ptolemy and a perfectly horrible stray. I expect you all heard it."

But Iris didn't look as if she had slept well at all. She was very pale and there were smudges under her eyes. And she still had that unexplainable look of excitement and tension.

Joyce Halstead said that when she went to

187

bed she slept like the dead. So did her husband. Doctor Bealey made no comment at all. His narrow pale face was bent over his plate as if he were concentrated on his food, but he wasn't missing anything, Antonia knew. He had a quick restless look that was expressed more in the rapid movements of his hands than in anything else. He was not, she decided, a comfortable person.

"Anyway, Antonia," Iris was saying, "you didn't get into any trouble last night." She addressed her remarks to the rest of the company. "Antonia has been doing extraordinary things. First she imagines she hears queer noises all night and then she falls down the stairs."

"Queer noises!" exclaimed Joyce Halstead, her eyes open wide. "How spooky! I expect it would be seagulls, wouldn't it? Or is the house haunted?"

"Not that we know of. We haven't been here long enough to find out. No, it was seagulls, of course. I've heard them myself on nights when there's a storm coming."

Antonia was aware of Ralph Bealey looking at her.

"Are you a sleep-walker?"

Iris answered for her. "She swears she isn't, but as I say, how does one know whether one sleep-walks or not? It's only other people who know."

"I'm sure I don't," Antonia said flatly.

She had a perfectly unreasonable feeling that everyone here, beneath their apparent friendliness, was really her enemy – Simon taking large mouthfuls of toast and chewing them up, his little moist full mouth moving rapidly, his eyes never meeting hers; Iris with her friendly concern and her slick smooth explanations, her quick flaming temper and her wariness; Ralph Bealey, too interested, too aware of her, his eyes glinting with excitement and meaning when he looked at her; Joyce and David Halstead not so much hostile as disturbed and disliking anything not quite normal.

If she were going to think things like that, she told herself uneasily, she really was becoming a little unbalanced. There was no reason on earth for any of these people to be hostile. It was purely her imagination.

"Such a malady," said Doctor Bealey suddenly, "could be brought on by a nervous condition. Have you been ill, Antonia?"

"I had 'flu rather badly before I left London," Antonia answered defensively.

"Ah! Perhaps your system is depleted."

"You don't look strong, dear," Joyce Halstead said sympathetically. "I'm sure this place will

189

do you all the good in the world. All that sea air coming up. So fresh and bracing. There's nothing like New Zealand air, I say."

She was being hypnotised into believing them. Part of her experiences had been natural simply explained things and the other part the result of an over-wrought imagination. That was the truth of it.

There was only one person she knew who would disagree and that was Henrietta Conroy who loved melodrama and persuaded herself that even Ethel, bashful and clumsy and giggling, must have her private life. As a consequence Henrietta's support really counted for nothing. She was alone.

"Poor Antonia," said Iris tenderly. "We're all talking about you, darling. Let's talk about something else. Are we all going to the flower festival? I don't think anyone has told you much about this, Antonia. There's a floral procession in the afternoon and at night a dance. There'll be literally millions of flowers, I believe."

"Christchurch is the garden city of New Zealand," Joyce Halstead said in her slightly geographical manner. "You want to see the gardens in the suburbs. Each house has one and of course they try to outdo one another. Then there's the right kind of climate—"

"When I go to my rooms later," Doctor Bealey interrupted, his eyes on Antonia, "I'd be delighted to drive you through the better parts of Christchurch. It's very English, I'm told."

"Splendid idea. Splendid," Simon said, for once looking at the company with bright eager eyes. "We haven't had time to take Antonia around at all. Iris and I — well, apart from everything else we've been busy with this place."

So poor Simon was a little jealous of Doctor Bealey. He was jumping at the suggestion that his attention should be diverted from Iris — if it had ever been seriously on her. Poor Simon. It wasn't comfortable loving someone as possessively as that, especially when one was a little slow and simple and one's beloved quick and restless and impatient. For Simon's sake, she thought, she would go with Doctor Bealey. But the proposal gave her no pleasure at all. She would be glad to be home again.

Doctor Bealey drove well. His car was new. He had only had it four days and had gone up to Mount Cook to run it in. It was coincidence that he should have met Iris and Simon there.

"Iris told me she had met you in Auckland," Antonia said.

"Yes. At a party. I remembered her, of

course. One does. She's so distinctive with that pale hair. She isn't beautiful, but what is it about her?"

Antonia knew what he meant. Iris's small sharply featured face with its crown of pussy willow hair hadn't beauty so much as a kind of force, a compelling quality that made one certainly remember her.

"At that time she was nursing old Miss Mildmay and she was pretty tired. She had insisted on doing the nursing herself, I believe, although it was a hopeless case."

There was a picture in Antonia's mind of the grave in Auckland and the rain-spattered card 'In loving and sorrowful memory. Iris.' That was another role for Iris, and one in which Antonia had difficulty in imagining her. But if she had nursed Aunt Laura with devotion she deserved something better than a husband whom she didn't love. For Antonia found it quite impossible to imagine Iris returning Simon's passionate devotion.

They drove round the bay with its curling white waves, and across the flat marshy farmland towards the city. Ralph Bealey proved a well-informed companion. He could name all the native trees in the gardens, the rata, the matapo, the plumed toi toi, the clematis spreading its tendrils over garden walls, and the beautiful drooping crimson fuchsias with their blossoms shaped like ballet dancers. But the gardens were predominantly English with their rosebeds and smooth lawns and borders of marigold, phlox and mignonette. There were flowers everywhere as if the early settlers had been more concerned with their seeds and rose cuttings than their livestock and household goods.

Antonia told herself she should have enjoyed the drive, but when they reached the heart of the city and the cathedral spire laid its pointed shadow over the square she sighed with relief. What was it about this dark, serious, probably brilliant young man that she didn't like, that was even slightly repellent to her? She could never forget the queer unreasonable thrill of fear that had gone through her when she had opened her eyes the previous afternoon and had seen him bending over her. It was as if a nightmare had become real — yet what was there in the least nightmarish about this suave well-mannered young man? It wasn't fair to judge him from that distorted half-awake impression she had of him.

"If anyone is unkind to you," he said suddenly, "you must tell me."

Antonia looked at him in astonishment.

"What a funny thing to say."

"I mean it."

"But apart from being old enough to look after myself, why should I tell you?"

"Because I'm concerned for you. I like you."

Antonia was intensely uncomfortable.

"That's nice of you. But—"

He laid his hand on her knee.

"No buts, my dear. I liked you the moment I saw you in the plane the other day."

Antonia drew quickly away, making her sudden animation an excuse to move herself from his hand.

"Was it coincidence that you were on the same plane that day?"

His brows lifted.

"But, of course. A lucky one, but a coincidence nevertheless. Did you think I was following you? But how should I have known of your arrival quite apart from who you were?"

His logic defeated her. And yet, stubbornly, she was not convinced. He smiled his flat smile that neither lifted nor turned down the corners of his mouth.

"I admit I found out later who you were. That's why I was so elated at meeting Iris and Simon at Mount Cook. Another coincidence. Doesn't all this seem significant to you?"

"I can't see any particular significance in it," Antonia said dampingly. "Thank you for the drive."

"Wait a minute, you're lunching with me, of course."

"I'm sorry, I can't. I have an appointment."

"Really?"

"Why do you suppose I should say that if I hadn't?" she asked in irritation that he didn't believe her lie.

"Then I shall drive you home after it. I'll meet you here."

There seemed no alternative to that. Antonia weakly agreed. She had the feeling that it was uselss to try to deceive Doctor Ralph Bealey. Somehow he would be shadowing her, aware of what she was doing. In spite of her common sense she couldn't shake off the instinct that beneath his suave exterior there was something queer, something perhaps perverted, or even evil.

She walked about the streets absently, looking into shop windows, reading names on glass doors. The city was too new to have any real interest or atmosphere. There were no dark mysterious archways, no blind beggars in doorways, no unexpected treasures behind dusty window panes. It was all new, clean, thriving and safe. Completely safe. Yet the discomfort she had felt in Ralph Bealey's presence persisted, and she felt more uneasy and apprehensive than she had ever felt in a continental city or in dark London lanes.

When suddenly she saw the name Dougal
Conroy, LL.B., Barrister and Solicitor, on a
brass nameplate an impulse took her quickly
into the office.

A thin middle-aged woman with a foxy face
and heavily rimmed glasses was coming out of
an inner room.

She said "Yes?" in a high sharp voice. "Did
you want Mr. Conroy?"

"Yes, please. I'm afraid I haven't an appointment. My name's Antonia Webb."

She was conscious that the woman gave her
a sharp interested look. Then she took her
neatly dressed flat body into the inner room
again. A moment later she emerged with Dougal
behind her.

"Antonia?" His voice held a question, almost
an apprehensive one.

She laughed. "It's all right. It's just necessary
for me to have a lunch appointment, so I wondered if it could be with you."

"Certainly." He looked at his watch. She was
aware of the slightly pursed mouth of the
woman before she slipped into her own room.
Good heavens, did all these women run Dougal's
life for him?

"Dougal, for heaven's sake don't be polite
about it! If it isn't convenient, say so."

196

"Of course it's convenient." But he still looked sober, his eyes searching hers. "Is there anything wrong?"

"No, nothing at all. I needed a lunch appointment. I'm using you. Do you mind?"

He didn't answer that. He said, "How's your ankle?"

"Oh, almost well."

"You're on it too much, I should think. I can't give you long because I have to go to court, but I usually have a sandwich about now."

"Then that's what we'll have. A sandwich and a glass of milk." She lowered her voice. "Who was that woman?"

"Miss Fox. My secretary."

"How delicious! She looks *exactly* like her name — as if she goes preying on chicken runs at night?"

He smiled. "Can't you be serious?"

"And you're her special chicken, I can see that. Look out she doesn't eat you one day. Yes, of course I can be serious. But not now, please. I've got to laugh or go nuts."

"What's happened?"

"Oh, nothing, really. It's all inside me, somehow. I think Iris must be right. I'm a schizophrenic or something."

She insisted that they have nothing more

197

than the sandwich and milk, and perched on stools over a glass-topped table she told him she had to meet Doctor Bealey again in an hour.

"I wish you'd go home again," he said emphatically. She looked at him in unbelief.

"To England?"

"England, if you like. Australia, America. Anywhere but here."

"Dougal!" The terrible thing was that he looked so in earnest over it, as if he acutely wanted her to go away. "Is this for my good or yours?"

"I don't know how it could conceivably be for mine."

"Ah, but it could. Your mother told me you didn't like red-headed women. I suppose my hair is red." She held a lock in front of her eyes and stared at it mournfully. "It could be called a rich brown."

"Antonia! This is no time for being coy! What I'm trying to tell you—"

"Coy! Me! Don't you dare say that. I've never been coy in my life. I'm telling you now I won't go away until I've found out what's been going on at the Hilltop, that light in the window, the crying, the grey hair I found, why I slipped on the stairs, why they all want to persuade me I'm a sleep-walker."

"If you'd only listen a minute," said Dougal, raising his voice, "I'd tell you—"

"How *could* I go away? Me, supposed to write articles and running away from something that might really be a story! Why, I've practically made Simon admit he gives Bella the brandy, and Gussie knows something that I'll get out of him before I'm a day older."

"If you don't go away," said Dougal with sudden quiet distinctness, "you might not *be* a day older."

"Why, there you are!" came a voice behind them. Antonia swung round to see Ralph Bealey standing smiling his flat smile and looking from her to Dougal with an expression that, for him, was probably pleasure. "I was just going to snatch a bite of lunch myself. May I join you?"

"Of course," said Antonia in a far-off voice. (So he was shadowing her, as she had suspected.) Dougal said nothing.

Ralph Bealey pulled out a stool and sat down. he took out a cigarette as he waited for his order to be taken.

"Do you mind if I smoke?"

"Not at all," said Antonia. Had Dougal suddenly lost his tongue? He might at least be civil even if he had the same unexplained feeling of panic as she had in Ralph Bealey's presence.

"Did you have any patients, Doctor Bealey?" she asked politely.

"No, I'm not completely organised yet."

"Tell me," said Dougal suddenly in the kind of voice he probably used for cross-examination, "what made you decide to come to Christchurch to practise?"

"Now, that's an involved question. Shall I say that chiefly I liked the prospects?"

"Ah, it wasn't a personal reason."

"If you mean, was any particular person involved, no. As it affects my future life, of course — well, I like the thought of making a home here."

Dougal gave him his level frankly assessing look. He drained his glass of milk.

"Antonia, will you call and see me at my office tomorrow morning. There are one or two things I'd like to discuss."

Antonia was surprised.

"Tomorrow's the floral procession."

"Before that starts. Say eleven o'clock."

"All right. Do you have to go now?"

"Yes. I'm in court all afternoon, otherwise I'd ask you to see me later. I'm sorry I have to rush off."

"Look out for that fox!" called Antonia. She spoke lightly, but she had to crush her impulse to run after him and beg him to take her with him. She was being purely childish, afraid of being left alone with Ralph Bealey in broad daylight.

"He's a nice young man," Ralph observed.

"Is he?" said Antonia with apparent indifference.

She was conscious of Ralph's quick glance. Now he was being inquisitive. Close-set dark eyes gave him an appearance of suspicion and meanness. Perhaps she judged Ralph unfairly when she judged him by his eyes.

"Don't you think so?"

"Oh, I don't know. We usually fight."

Why was Dougal suddenly getting into a panic about her? And what had he been going to say to her? Now she wouldn't know until tomorrow morning, and that was a long way off.

Ralph said he was going to drive her home a different way. He went through the hillside suburb of Cashmere with its brilliant rock gardens, its houses perched one above the other like birds on a rail. In a short time they left the houses behind and came on to the bare sheep-cropped hillside. The road wound like a smooth grey scar between rocky outcrops and low round hills. In the afternoon sunlight the rocks had a hard glare, the everlasting tussocks a golden shine. Beneath them the Canterbury plains lay like a map, stretching in blue shadows to the mountains in the west.

In spite of the brilliant sunshine the wind was chilly. It had an infinitely lonely sound when, at the highest point of the road, Ralph stopped the car and opened the door for Antonia to get out.

"Come and look at the view," he invited.

The wind whipped round her skirts as she followed him to a ledge of rocks that overhung a steep drop into the valley below. On this side of the hill the blue waters of the bay shone like a jewel and the hillsides were deeply green with native bush. It was odd, the bleak clear bony sun-dried slopes on one side, and the sparkling water and lush vegetation on this.

"These hills have volcanic origin," Ralph was saying. "The bay was the crater of the volcano. It's difficult to imagine, isn't it? Those yachts sailing on what should be a sea of lava." He put his hand on her arm. "Don't let me be like Joyce Halstead and give you a geographical lecture. Antonia, I've brought you up here to ask you something."

She turned to look at him. In spite of the wind his hair was not disturbed. It lay flat and smooth on his head. His profile was pale and clear-cut, his nose long and with a domineering look. He looked completely self-possessed and quite alien to this barren hillside.

Dougal's hair, Antonia thought irrelevantly, would have been all over his head like a straw broom.

Now she knew what it was about Ralph's skin that she didn't like. It had the appearance of not having been in the sun or fresh air enough.

She had an uneasy feeling of in reality standing on the lip of an active volcano. Lonely sheep calls came across the valleys. The wind blew her hair in her eyes.

"What do you want to ask me?" she said levelly.

"I want to know if you will marry me."

She took a step away from him in sheer surprise.

"Ralph! But good heavens—"

"You think I'm a bit rapid? But I always make quick decisions and they're usually right. I — I want you very much."

His hesitation over his last statement could not conceivably have been caused by bashfulness because he was least of all a bashful person. So it had a slightly phoney ring, as if it were added for good measure, because a girl expected that kind of thing. Yet his hand gripping her arm was bruising her.

"Oh, Ralph! I'm sorry! But really, I don't feel in the least like that about you. No, it's no use dissembling. I must just thank you very much and refuse."

His eyes began to sparkle in a queer way. Probably he was a man of deep-hidden passions, like the volcano they were standing on. Perhaps her refusal had been a bit curt. But she had to be completely honest right away. One couldn't fool with a man like Ralph Bealey.

"Are you quite sure about that?" he asked.

"I'm afraid so. I make quick decisions, too. Truly Ralph, I'm awfully grateful to you, but it's just no use."

"I've hurried you too much," he said.

She shook her head. "No. It would make no difference, now or any other time." Again she regretted her curtness. "I'm sorry," she added helplessly.

It seemed, crazily, that there was almost pity in his face, not for himself but for her. Was this lonely place and this strange cold proposal of marriage making her unable to interpret his reactions?

"I'm sorry, too," he said briefly. His hand on her arm seemed to move nearer the ledge of rock. But that was imagination, of course. He wasn't, in his deep disappointment, going to fling her into the valley below!

Then he said, as if they had been doing

nothing more than looking at the view, "Come along. Let's go."

In the car another inconsequential thought came to Antonia. It couldn't possibly have been for her money that Ralph Bealey wanted to marry her because four thousand pounds to him, with this new expensive car and apparently everything he needed financially would be chicken-feed. No, he was the unlikely victim of a sudden infatuation that had begun that day in the plane. For that reason she had to be sorry for him.

With Dougal urging her to go away and Ralph wanting to marry her she had had quite a day. It would be good to get home and relax.

But that, she found, was not to be possible. For when they arrived there was consternation in the house. Gussie had not come home from fishing. His lines and bait had been found on a rock lapped dangerously by the incoming tide, but there was no sign of Gussie. It looked as if he had been tragically drowned.

# XV

Because he had been in court all afternoon Dougal didn't see Miss Fox until he was almost ready to go home. Then she came bustling in with letters for signature. He knew at once that the thing that had been on her mind all afternoon was Antonia Webb.

He said resignedly, "Well! Did you approve of her?"

To his surprise Miss Fox exclaimed enthusiastically, "She's lovely. Quite lovely. You never told me."

Did one discuss one's client's appearance with one's secretary? Apparently when the secretary was Miss Fox one did.

"She's a good-looking girl," he agreed. "Personally—" No, he was damned if he was going to explain to Miss Fox that she was not his type. Next thing the nosey little woman would be ferreting out of him what his type was. The quiet dark-haired girl with the serene eyes.... Antonia's eyes hadn't a chance to be serene. They were always sparkling with excitement or courage or anger. Or fear.

"Mr. Conroy, don't you think it would be wise to tell her the truth?"

Dougal leaned back uncomfortably. Miss Fox had a way of startling him with her acute perceptiveness.

"What, are you advising a solicitor to expressly disobey a testator's instructions?"

"The circumstances warrant it."

"I was not aware that you knew the circumstances."

The end of Miss Fox's sharp nose quivered.

"I know that she's living with Mr. and Mrs. Mildmay and they're an odd couple, to say the least. I don't trust either of them."

"Come now, surely Simon—"

"He's been hoodwinked by a woman. I've no patience with him."

Dougal raised his thick fair brows.

"If marrying the woman you love is to be hoodwinked—"

"She's posing and he can't see through her. I'm finding out more about her. She wasn't a stewardess for nothing. She was probably getting out of England as unobtrusively as possible."

Again Dougal was startled, this time by the fact that there may have been more than a flavour of truth in Miss Fox's allegations.

"Now, Miss Fox, you're romancing. You haven't a shadow of proof."

"I'll get it," said Miss Fox grimly. "What's more, I'm making a good guess that there'll be an exhumation order before this estate is wound up."

"Good God! What are you getting into your head now? Laura Mildmay died of a stroke. Have a look at the death certificate. But of course you've done that."

Miss Fox shook her head obstinately.

"Doctors have been fooled before."

"Hardly over this type of illness. Anyway, if it eases your mind I've decided to act completely unethically and show Miss Webb the will. As it happens, I agree with you in this matter, even if the trustee doesn't. She's so near her twenty-fourth birthday (apparently Miss Mildmay's interpretation of the age of discretion) that it's neither here nor there."

"Good!" said Miss Fox in tones of relief. "Good! Do it as soon as possible. The sooner the better."

# XVI

The white cat was always sitting in front of the bird cage. Iris would come into the hall and pick it up and fondle it, then absently let it escape from her arms and it would immediately go back to its position, a foot or so away from the flitting chattering birds, protected by their screen of fine wire netting. Simon, if he thought Iris was not within hearing, would suddenly lunge at it, saying, "Shoo! Shoo! Get away, you beast!" and the cat, its tail spread to a plume, would fly for the kitchen. But immediately after Simon had gone it would slink back again. It wanted to hypnotise the birds with its green stare, but they, secure in their cage, were gaily oblivious to its threat.

The white cat didn't know that Gussie, one of its tormentors, was missing. If it had had human intelligence would it have wondered how a shrewd wily boy like Gussie had come to fall in the sea?

Antonia's eyes were strained and tired from watching the little boats going out over the bay and nosing cautiously among the rocks. She knew that Bella, who was far more nervous that Gussie was up to some mischief than that he might be dead, had opposed sending for the police, but Iris had insisted. It was their duty, she urged, to do everything possible. Since all the evidence pointed to Gussie having slipped off the rock where he was fishing they had to have an immediate investigation.

"He'd fool you like that," Bella said. "He'd leave his stuff and be somewhere else altogether, up to no good. Ah, he's a little devil though he is my own son."

But she was saying that to convince herself, Antonia guessed. Beneath her indignation she was desperately frightened. She had been drinking again, too. There was the smell of brandy on her breath and her efforts to prepare the dinner were haphazard, to say the least. It was fortunate that Henrietta had sent Ethel up, otherwise they may not have eaten at all, and Iris, with her reputation for cuisine to keep up now that she had her first guests, could not afford that.

Tradesmen had come, too, with patterns of

wallpaper and carpets, and Iris had spread them out on the floor in the hall and called for opinions.

The men were all down at the beach helping in the search for Gussie, so Iris had only Joyce and Antonia to consult. Joyce was flattered to be asked for her views and entered into a loud animated discussion as to the virtues of a plain buff-coloured carpet as opposed to a floral design.

"I think perhaps the buff will be best," Iris decided at last. "I'm having bright blue shutters and deck chairs on the terraces and tubs of red geraniums, so perhaps a quiet colour when one comes inside will be more soothing. Don't you agree, Antonia?"

Antonia nodded absently. She couldn't rid herself of the feeling that these plans of Iris's were more fleeting than a summer, that the gaily coloured shutters and the little red tubs and the cool windy rooms would spring into flower for a season only, that it was all far too transient to make it worth while exercising any effort.

Iris looked at her sharply.

"Now, Antonia! Don't let that fertile imagination of yours run away with you. We're all upset about Gussie, but he'll turn up, you'll see. There's no point in sitting brooding. Is there, Joyce?"

Joyce Halstead obviously admired Iris very much. She nodded vigorously.

"You're absolutely right. If the kid's to be found the men will find him." She lowered her voice. "Personally, I can't think that he'd be much loss. Nasty little brute, wasn't he? The kind that would break his poor mother's heart."

(If Gussie were dead, was his death accidental or deliberate? That was the question that tormented Antonia.)

"When Simon comes back," Iris went on, "I'll get him to mix that new cocktail. He practised one while you were in town today, Antonia. It's quite something. Isn't it Joyce?"

Joyce giggled.

"Guaranteed to make you sleep. I only woke up after lunch when there was the fuss about Gussie."

"Now that's an idea," said Iris. "One of Simon's cocktails might give you a very good night, Antonia. Is that the men I can hear coming now? I wonder if they have any news."

The three men came in rather wearily. Both Simon's and David Halstead's faces were flushed with the exertion of climbing up the hill, but Ralph Bealey's remained colourless although there were beads of perspiration on his upper lip.

"No luck," said David Halstead. "If you ask

me, it's a blind and the kid's gone off on his own bat somewhere."

"It's too dark to search any more," Ralph Bealey said in his precise way, his words neatly clipped as if he were making a diagnosis. "If the boy's fallen in the sea he can't be alive now. If he's gone somewhere he'll be picked up soon enough."

"Then we can't do anything more," said Iris. It seemed as if her voice held relief. Probably, secretly, she was glad to be rid of Gussie and his awkward spying ways. Gussie knew something she preferred him not to tell, too. Probably it suited her very well that he had disappeared.

"His poor mother," Joyce Halstead murmured.

Simon said nothing at all. He sat leaning forward in his chair, his head bent, his big hands hanging loose. He didn't look up at anyone.

"Conroy was helping us," David Halstead observed. "My word, that man can handle a boat." He began to chuckle. "That mother of his has the most fantastic notions. She stood up to her ankles in water saying the boy had been murdered, one must start looking for motives and so on."

"She's a scream," said his wife.

"Well, at least she provided a bit of humour."

"Motives," murmured Iris seriously. "Well, Gussie did tease Ptolemy last night. I might easily have murdered him for that. At the time, anyway. Simon, wouldn't you murder anyone who interfered with your birds?"

"Eh?" Simon lifted his head, shaking it muzzily. "My birds! I can't say I'd exactly pat 'em on the back."

"That's the only motive I can think of," said Iris. "Oh, bother the little wretch, causing all this fuss and bother. Simon, fix us some drinks. We need them badly. And take Bella one, too."

Before the drinks were ready – Simon was industriously shaking the cocktail shaker while he got sundry reminders as to what ingredients he had used earlier in the day – Antonia went to find Bella. She was wishing with surprising acuteness that Dougal had come up to the Hilltop with the other men. He could have talked to Bella with her now. As it was, she had the little tearless frightened-face woman alone.

"They haven't found him?" she demanded the moment Antonia came in.

"Not yet. But don't give up hope. It's far too early to give up hope."

Bella shook her head slowly. Her eyes were far-off, dark with their thoughts.

"He's gone," she whispered. She made an

effort to straighten her narrow shoulders. "Well, they did say he would come to a bad end. I've said it to him myself many a time. And so has his father," she added, her voice suddenly trembling.

"Bella," said Antonia, "is there any reason that Gussie might have wanted to run away? From this house, I mean?"

Bella looked up at her quickly, then away. She got out a handkerchief and blew her thin nose vigorously.

"What a thing to say!" she said behind her handkerchief. "It was lonely here for a boy, of course."

"You know I don't mean that. Was he frightened of anything?"

"Frightened! My goodness, no, you couldn't frighten that boy." Bella's voice was loud and derisive, too derisive, Antonia thought. "I wish you could of."

"He said he knew something. I think he was coming up to tell me last night, but — he was stopped." She had been going to say that Iris had stopped him, but she changed her mind. It was better for these as yet unfounded suspicions to be quite impersonal.

Bella's mouth hung open slightly. She looked extraordinarily like a caught fish, red-eyed and gasping.

"He did the boots this morning," she said at last. "He didn't go down to the beach till daylight. At least they were done when I got up, so he must have done them before he went. If he'd have wanted to run away he'd have done it in the dark."

"Then there's no reason for his wanting to run away?"

Bella turned her head with a swift movement this way and that. Suddenly she clutched Antonia's arm and whispered, "He had something. He found something and hid it and even I can't find it now. I don't know what—"

Her voice stopped abruptly as the door opened and Ralph Bealey came in with a glass in his hand.

"Oh, there you are, Antonia," he said. His voice was genial. "Bella, I've been detailed to bring you this concoction with Mr. Mildmay's compliments. It'll make you sleep and in the morning that shocking rascal of yours will have turned up."

Bella took the glass. She managed a dim smile. Her thin nostrils twitched at the odour of the liquor and already her eyes were glistening.

"Come along, Antonia, and get yours," Ralph said. "It's really surprisingly good. Simon shakes a clever cocktail. Crazy hour to drink it, of course, but the girls all say it'll help to make them sleep."

Antonia said good night to Bella and went with him. There was nothing else to do. It was infuriating that Ralph had interrupted Bella's first confidence. Now she might never persuade the woman to talk again.

"I don't think anything will make me sleep," she said, going back into the dining-room.

"Really!" said Ralph. "Then I must give you some sleeping tablets. I have some with me. I'll give you the bottle and you can take one if this drink doesn't fix you."

"What a good idea," said Iris. "Antonia's looking shockingly tired. But try Simon's drink first, darling. It's really frightfully potent."

Simon handed her the glass from the top of the cocktail cabinet and lifted his own.

"Here's mud in your eye," he said dejectedly.

They were all drinking with the seriousness of alcoholics. Simon wordlessly lifted the shaker and indicated that he would refill any glasses. Iris suddenly held hers out.

"Damn that boy!" she declared. "I feel like getting drunk. One thing, whether he's found or not, we all go in to see the floral procession and to the dance tomorrow night. We can't go into mourning for Gussie's pranks."

Her hand as she lifted her glass was shaking

slightly. She was more disturbed than she had admitted. She would feel that this was a bad omen for the success of her venture. People would remember. They would say about the Hilltop, "But wasn't there a small boy who drowned there?" It was bad luck for Iris and Simon. It couldn't mean anything else to them as they had had no affection for Gussie.

Antonia didn't think that anyone had shared her feeling of horror as she had watched the little boats going out over the glittering sea, a horror that still clung to her. It appeared, however, that someone did share something at least of her feelings, for a few minutes later Dougal Conroy telephoned and asked to speak to her.

"You're not alone?" he queried.

She could scarcely have been less alone. Simon had gone over to mutter and whisper to his birds who were too sleepy to respond. Joyce Halstead, in the dining-room, was talking in her loud voice, and Iris, her glass still in her hand, was moving restlessly about, always within hearing.

"No. I'm not. Why?"

"Oh, nothing. It's a bad thing about Gussie, isn't it?"

"Awful. Dougal, do you think—"

"I'd hate to repeat what Mother thinks." His voice had a way that nothing else had of giving her reassurance. "Actually, it doesn't look too good. He was a reckless little creature. It looks as if he's slipped, or something. The police are checking every avenue. How are things up there?"

"Oh – not very happy. We're all having a new cocktail Simon's mixed. Why don't you come up and have one?"

"I think not tonight. You won't forget that appointment in the morning, will you?"

"Certainly not." She wanted to add that she was extremely curious about it, but again Iris was in her vicinity and something made her hold her tongue.

"Good. There's nothing more can be done to-night. You'd better get to bed."

"Dougal, it was nice of you to ring."

"Oh, never mind that." She could visualise the slight embarrassment in his eyes. Suddenly she felt light-hearted and cheerful. That cock-tail of Simon's was potent.

"How's the fox?"

"Well – not chicken-stealing, anyway."

"Good night, Dougal."

"Good night. Oh, by the way."

"Yes?"

He lowered his voice. Probably his mother or sharp-eared giggling Ethel was in earshot.

"I'd lock my door tonight if I were you."

"Dougal!" She couldn't keep the astonishment out of her voice. And now it was intolerable that she couldn't ask him what he meant.

"It's probably foolishness on my part," she heard him saying in his slightly embarrassed voice. "But do it, please."

That was why he had rung her. All the other polite chatter had led up to it. Antonia found it both comforting and disturbing to know that he shared her vague suspicions and fears. She intended to obey him religiously. As a matter of fact, it would add greatly to her peace of mind if her door were locked. Especially since Simon's cocktail seemed to have made her extraordinarily sleepy and she wanted to tumble into her bed and completely relax.

She was not allowed to do this, however. She was scarcely undressed before there was a tap on the door and the knob was tried.

"Antonia," called Iris's voice. "You've locked your door, darling. Are you as nervous as that?"

Antonia hurriedly turned the key and let Iris in. Iris's cheeks were flushed and she looked very slightly intoxicated.

"I'm sorry. I just thought—"

"I know, darling. Don't bother to explain. You feel safer that way. Well, I'm sure I do, too. The thought of you tumbling down the stairs breaking your neck gives me the horrors."

"Iris, once and for all, I do *not* sleep-walk."

Iris looked at her with slightly glazed eyes.

"Then explain to me, will you, what you have been up to."

"Explain to you!" Antonia exclaimed heatedly. "*You* explain to me why that seaweed was on the stairs the other night, why the telephone rang, why someone cried in the room in the other wing, why the light went out when I knocked, and why I found that grey hair. And why Gussie knew something he wanted to tell."

Iris's eyes were open wide.

"Antonia!" she said in shocked tones. "But, darling, you're suffering from hallucinations. Really you are. You must have a consultation with Ralph tomorrow. I insist. You can see him here or at his rooms."

"Isn't it a little odd," Antonia began (she was trying to speak with great distinctness, but it was difficult because she was so extraordinarily sleepy), "that Doctor Bealey who you insist is such a brilliant doctor and likely to notice any peculiarity about a person should want to marry me if I suffer from hallucinations." She paused. "I'm sure sanity would be the first thing a doctor would want in a wife."

She lifted her heavy eyelids with her fingers and held them, her fingers spread over her hot forehead. Iris was standing quite still, her mouth open as if she had begun to say something in unbelief. Antonia was aware that this should have been significant, but couldn't think why.

"Did Ralph — ask you to marry him?" she finally said.

"Yes, in an awful place up on the top of a hill. The wind howling round. I refused, of course."

"You refused?"

"Indeed, I did. Why, I don't even know him, much less feel that way about him. As a matter of fact," she finished confidentially, "I find him rather repellent. Don't you?"

Iris didn't answer for a while. Her eyes were glittering again as if this information had made her throw off the effects of Simon's drink. There was a look of intolerable excitement in her eyes.

"Repellent," she said at last, slowly. "Well — it's a matter of taste. Actually, darling, I think you were wise."

"I know I was." Antonia sat on the edge of the bed. "Lord, that was some drink of Simon's, or else I'm allergic to that particular mixture. Do you mind if I go to sleep?"

Iris gave a little high laugh.

"Well, how funny, and I've brought you Ralph's sleeping pills. Look, I'll just put them beside your bed in any case. Good night, darling. And by all means lock your door if it makes you feel safer."

Lock your door, Antonia thought tiredly. Yes, Dougal had told her to. She must do what Dougal asked. That was the one important thing in this whole crazy business.

She turned the key again and went back to bed. It seemed she had hardly switched off the light before she was asleep.

Someone was rapping at her door and calling, "Antonia! Wake up and open the door! You're wanted on the telephone!"

Antonia opened her eyes and shook her head muzzily. Telephone — that was a danger signal. It was a trick. Someone would lure her out somewhere, or she would fall down the stairs.

"Antonia!" called Iris. "Dougal Conroy wants to speak to you. It's after eleven o'clock."

Antonia shot upright. For a moment her head throbbed as if it would burst. Then it settled down into a dull perplexing ache. After eleven o'clock, Iris had said. But how could she have slept so long?

"Antonia, are you all right?" There seemed to be alarm in Iris's voice. Then Antonia could hear the rumble of Simon's voice. She got out of bed, dragged on a wrap and walking rather

223

dizzily to the door turned the key.

"I must have overslept," she said. It was clear that Iris had spoken the truth for it was broad daylight.

"You certainly have," said Iris. "I said you weren't to be disturbed, but I didn't know you had this appointment with Dougal at eleven. Run down and speak to him. He sounds in a bit of a flap."

That was true. Antonia had never heard Dougal so agitated.

"I say, are you all right?"

"Of course I am." She rubbed her hand over her eyes, trying to clear her vision. "At least, I've slept far too long and feel like nothing on earth. But I'm all right."

His voice came back in deep indignation. "Good grief! Do you mean to say I've been sitting here worrying like hell as to what has happened to you and you've merely slept in."

His indignation roused her more than anything else. She could imagine him sitting there with his blue fierce eyes and his ruffled hair and she began to smile.

"I'm terribly sorry. I can't think how I came to sleep like that."

"You didn't take anything, did you?"

"No. They gave me sleeping pills but I didn't need any. It must have been that cocktail of

Simon's. I thought I had a better head for liquor." Abruptly her memory was returning. "Is there any news of Gussie?"

"Not yet. Do you mean to say you don't know that, either?"

"I haven't had time to find out." She added pityingly, "Poor Bella."

"Never mind Bella now," he said rather callously. "When can you get in to see me?"

"A little later. When I wake up properly."

"Antonia!" came Iris's voice from behind her. "Don't make another appointment with Dougal yet. We're all having early lunch and going in to see the procession. Dougal will have to wait till tomorrow."

"Sorry," said Antonia into the telephone, "I was just listening to Iris. We seem to be getting ready to go to the procession."

"And then there's the dance tonight," went on Iris. "You won't have time to see Dougal today. Make your appointment for this time tomorrow. I'll see you get there."

Iris had come into the hall and was standing near the bird cage with Ptolemy in her arms. She had on a yellow linen dress. The white cat against her breast and the colour of her dress and her smooth pale hair made her seem cool and pure and a little remote.

"Tomorrow morning, Dougal," said Antonia,

225

a little hypnotically. There was something about the heaviness of her head and the confusing voices that made her unable to think at all.

"I'd rather—" Dougal's voice was suddenly drowned by an uproar behind her. Ptolemy had sprung out of Iris's arms and made a leap at the bird cage. The wires vibrated from his impact and the birds flew about, twittering madly.

"I can't hear a thing," shouted Antonia into the telephone. "I'll see you tomorrow."

Simon, hearing the noise, had come rushing into the hall.

"Now, it's all right, Simon," Iris insisted. "There isn't a bird hurt. If anyone's hurt it's Ptolemy, the poor sweet silly."

"—today," Antonia thought she heard Dougal saying.

"I'll ring you again," she told him. "There's too much noise going on here."

She hung up and turned to see Simon, red-faced and anxious, poking his thick finger through the wires of the cage and twittering soothingly to the ruffled birds.

"Now, darling, don't be so fussed," said Iris impatiently.

"But it's bad for them. They shouldn't be frightened like that. Look, even Johnnie won't come on my finger now. You've got him too nervous."

"I!" Iris said indignantly. "Why, I'm doing my best to keep the peace. I tell you, Ptolemy will learn he can't get them and then he'll leave them alone." She put her slim arm across Simon's broad back. "Don't be such a big silly!"

But Simon sulked. He took no notice of her. He whispered, "Pretty boy! Pretty boy!" and tried to entice the wary yellow bird on to his finger.

Iris followed Antonia out of the hall.

"I've asked Bella to make coffee for you, darling," she said. "Isn't Simon a baby! Really! Oh, what did you arrange with Dougal?"

"What you suggested. Tomorrow morning."

"Ah, good. Does he want to give you some money or something?"

"I don't know why he wants me."

"Well, it will keep until tomorrow. You know Gussie hasn't turned up yet, don't you. I've told Bella to go off for a few days, but she says she has nowhere to go, poor soul."

(So she would stay here sitting in the big lonely kitchen listening to the everlasting grieving of the sea until one day her son's body was washed up on the sand.)

"Can't she be sent somewhere?" Antonia exclaimed in pity.

"I've offered to do that. Simon would willingly pay for her to go anywhere. But she prefers to stay. She thinks he'll come back, you know. But the police are almost certain he's been drowned. Everything points to it." For a moment her eyes were darkened with horror. Then she gave herself a little shake. "For God's sake, don't let us start brooding about it. We've got to be cheerful."

"What do you think it was that Gussie threatened to tell me the other night?"

Iris looked at her apprehensively. "Now," she warned, "don't you start talking that extraordinary nonsense like you did last night. I think that drink was affecting you." Then she went on lightly, "Oh, I shouldn't think Gussie had anything of importance to tell. Kids like to get secretive over trivial things. It's exhibitionism, that's all. And Gussie, as you know, was just about the world's worst exhibitionist. But I wish I hadn't slapped him, all the same, poor little devil."

Was there a note of hypocrisy in Iris's voice? Antonia felt too heavy and dull to think. She sat down and heard Iris's voice coming from what seemed a long way off.

"Antonia, you don't look a bit well. So tired. Really, darling, I insist that you see a doctor."

"It was Simon's cocktail," Antonia muttered.

"It's given me a hangover."

"But none of the rest of us has one and we all drank it." Iris laughed. "Poor Simon would be hurt. He's proud of that cocktail. We named it Waking Dream. Don't you think that's clever? Ah, here's Bella with your coffee. We're having lunch at twelve and leaving at one. Ralph is taking Simon and you and I in his car and the Halsteads are going on their own. I'll leave you now because I must help Bella. She just can't concentrate today."

Fifteen minutes later, when Antonia, wondering if she would feel any fresher after a cold bath, went upstairs she ran into Iris coming out of her room. Iris's face was concerned.

"Antonia, are you sure you didn't take any sleeping tablets last night?"

"Positive."

"Then where are they? This bottle was full last night." She held the bottle up between her fingers. "Look, it's a third empty now. There must be at least seven or eight gone."

"If I'd taken seven or eight," Antonia said patiently, "I'd hardly be alive to tell you now, would I?"

Iris looked a little shocked.

"No, I suppose you wouldn't. Ralph said three was absolutely the maximum dose. But you did sleep awfully late."

"It was Simon's cocktail," Antonia insisted wearily. Waking Dream. The name was so appropriate as to be humorous. She certainly felt as if she were in a waking dream. But why did Iris bother her about the sleeping tablets? She hadn't taken them and that was all there was to it.

"Well — never mind," Iris said. She didn't believe her. Antonia could see, but she suddenly apparently decided the matter was not worth arguing about. She returned the bottle to the bedside table and giving Antonia a rather odd look went out.

The bed was neatly made and the curtains drawn so that the cheerful sunshine streamed in. The sea lifted its innocent blue face to the horizon. At any moment now Gussie, a grubby starved-looking urchin, would come toiling up to the hillside from his morning fishing. Nothing of yesterday had happened. Ralph Bealey's queer cold proposal of marriage, Gussie's disappearance, Bella's interrupted confidence, Simon's new cocktail, the bottle of sleeping pills with a third of the sinister little yellow capsules missing. It was all a waking dream. Presently the mist over her brain would clear and she would be able to come back to reality.

Who would have taken the sleeping tablets? — if it were true that the bottle really had been full. And for what purpose?

# XVII

The lorries, wagons, handcarts and bicycles went slowly past, weighted down with their glowing burden of flowers. The great heads of the purple and blue hydrangeas, the roses and delphiniums and asters, and the dahlias, so brilliant that their colours hurt the eye, went by in a rainbowhued mass. Pretty girls in light dresses flung roses from baskets, clowns with garlands of flowers round their necks pranced by, children perched on the tops of flower-laden vehicles with blossoms trailing from their hands. The sky was blue, the air clean and crisp with early autumn.

It was as if one were drowning in flowers, as if the great soft crimson petals of the dahlias were pressed against one's face blotting out all sense and memory and leaving only this blurred warm delight.

Ralph Bealey had parked his car on a slight rise behind the mass of people lining the streets. Sitting in it they could see the festivities quite clearly. The radio was playing softly, and the colourful floats slipped past to the accompaniment of a Strauss waltz.

"Well," said Simon with simple delight. "This is wonderful."

"Those dahlias give me an idea," said Iris. "Do you think they would grow along the south wall at the Hilltop? They would be marvellous, those yellow and scarlets. Wouldn't they, Simon?"

"I suppose they would." He added uneasily, "I wonder if they've found any trace of Gussie."

Iris turned on him reproachfully. "Don't remind us of Gussie now, please. It's quite enough living in that atmosphere at home."

"You can't put it right out of your mind like that," Simon muttered.

Ralph turned his polite pale face.

"Iris is right, old man. We can't help by letting the thing haunt us. Isn't that so, Antonia?"

He looked at Antonia in the front seat. She sensed a double meaning in his words — he was referring as much to his refused offer of marriage as he was to Gussie. So he didn't intend to let that haunt him, either. He had a cold controlled mind that put events away in compartments and shut the door on them. He was a complete realist. She thought she would have liked him a little better had he been human enough to give her reproachful glances. But that would have been unendurable, too. She was aware that if her head had been clearer she would have been more conscious of the atmosphere in the car, Simon's uneasiness, Iris's slight but noticeable shortness of temper, as if she were suffering from acute tension, Ralph Bealey's peculiar calm that was almost triumph.

It was as if beneath their friendliness they all distrusted one another intensely. Antonia felt sure that had she been able to think more clearly she would have known why. The answer was just eluding her.

A group of girls on a truck went slowly past flinging roses at the watchers. The perfume drifted through the still air. From the radio in the car the Strauss waltz finished and the announcer's voice came seriously:

"We break this programme to make the following announcement: Would anyone knowing the whereabouts of the following missing person please notify the nearest police station."

They were broadcasting for Gussie, thought Antonia, startled. But the voice went on impersonally, "An elderly woman thought to be wearing a black hat and coat and carrying a small suitcase. She has grey hair, blue eyes, a bright complexion and is about five feet six inches in height. She will probably ask the time and the way to the railway station. Anyone seeing a woman answering to this description is particularly urged to get in touch with the police immediately, as she is of unsound mind and may be dangerous. We will repeat that announcement . . ."

Antonia exclaimed, "With a crowd like this the poor old soul will get completely lost."

No one answered. The complete silence in the car was suddenly significant. Instinctively Antonia turned her head and caught Iris's and Simon's expressions. Iris's teeth were biting her lower lip, the pupils of her eyes were darkened (like Ptolemy's when he watched Simon's birds) so that none of the green showed. Simon had his small ripe cherry mouth open in alarm that he made no effort to hide.

"Why, what's wrong?" Antonia asked lightly. Her heart had begun to beat violently with excitement. The answer — the answer that was always eluding her. Was this anything to do with it? "Do you know this woman?"

Iris let out her breath in a half laugh.

"She's a lunatic, didn't you hear him say? I'm just terrified of lunatics."

"May ask the time and the way to the railway

234

station," the announcer was repeating.

"In this crowd she may be anywhere," Iris said breathlessly.

"The fools! Why did they have to broadcast!" Simon burst out.

Ralph Bealey said smoothly, "Yes, it was rather foolish in the middle of this festival. People may get a bit panicky." He looked at Antonia with his flat smile. "It doesn't fit in, does it, a crazy woman and all this beauty. Like the earwig in the dahlia."

"Ralph, what a simile!" Iris exclaimed. "But apt, all the same. Bother that old creature, whoever she is. She's spoilt the procession for me." She shivered. "I just can't bear lunatics."

While listening to her an extraordinary thing was happening in Antonia's mind. It was as if she were seeing again in slow motion what had happened last night, Ralph leading her from the kitchen into the dining-room, Simon taking the single remaining cocktail from the cocktail cabinet and handing it to her, the last one, the one into which someone could so easily have put a sleeping powder, and saying dejectedly, because he would not be happy about drugging anyone, "Here's mud in your eye!"

They said one felt extraordinarily heavy and dull after taking a sleeping powder. Obviously that was what had happened to her. But the dose wouldn't have been meant to be lethal. No, it was simpler than that. They merely wanted to prevent her from seeing Dougal that morning.

Again why? What was so important about seeing him tomorrow instead of today? Was it that tomorrow would be too late?

The new clarity of Antonia's brain didn't tell her how it would be too late. It didn't emphasise that it might be because she wouldn't be alive. How could it be so fantastic a thing? True, she had slipped on the stairs, she had been drugged, sleeping tablets had been put within her reach, people's minds had been deliberately fostered in the belief that she might do some unbalanced thing. But *why* was all this done? She had only suspicions, not knowledge like Gussie.

Gussie! A shiver, a distinct feeling of her hair standing on end, came over her. Could it be that Gussie's absence was deliberate, was engineered?

"Go away," Dougal had said. And later, "Lock your door at night." She had thought he was influenced by his mother's inventive imagination, but perhaps he, too, had some knowledge, dangerous knowledge, that he had been going to pass on to her this morning. Something strangely connected with the light in the empty wing, the crying at night and now a poor old woman whose brain was affected.

Her hand was on the handle of the door. Cautiously she pressed it and the door began to open.

"Tonia, what are you doing?" Iris cried. Before she could do more than put her foot out of the door Ralph had put his thin hard fingers round her wrist, holding her in a snare.

"Let me go, please!" she said, breathing quickly, trying to keep her voice normal. "I want to get out. One can see the procession better outside."

"You mustn't stand on that ankle," said Ralph.

"No darling. You mustn't," Iris echoed.

Antonia felt panic rushing in her.

"Good heavens, if I can dance I can stand for five minutes."

"That's just the point, darling, If you're coming with us tonight you must rest that foot today. You know it still swells."

Iris was leaning slightly forward. Antonia could smell her perfume, Chanel No. 5. The expensive perfume that someone had sprinkled mischievously about her room. She could see her silvery pale hair wreathed round her small head, a halo for her taut white face. She was aware of the tenseness in Simon's big body, the almost unendurable closeness of Ralph's flat-lipped face, and of the pain of his hard grip on her wrist. She had a wild desire to scream as someone had screamed when she had fallen the other night. To scream like a trapped rabbit so that people would turn to stare and she would be able to say, "I am being kept here against my will."

The gay vehicles with their fragrant burdens continued to glide past. There were outbursts of clapping and cheers. The air was full of sunshine and flowers. And somewhere a poor witless old woman was seeking the way to the railway station to catch an imaginary train. Who was she? Had she any connection with the people at the Hilltop, or was that Antonia's imagination becoming distorted again?

Ralph Bealey leaned across her and closed the car door. He loosed his grip on her wrist, giving her hand a little pat with his cool dry fingers.

"I think we'll go now," said Iris. "We've seen practically everything." She was still sitting on the edge of the seat, but her voice was quite normal. "I have a lot to do and Antonia can put her foot up for the afternoon. Don't you think that's a good idea, Ralph?"

"Excellent. We might try cold compresses."

The time for cold compresses was long past, Antonia wanted to say. But all at once she was speechless, as if this sudden solicitude of theirs was for someone who was dying.

Then, "For God's sake, let's go!" Simon burst out, and Ralph pressed the starter of the car.

As soon as they got home Iris said she had a lot of telephoning to do and shut herself in her bedroom. Antonia wanted to ring Dougal, but perforce had to wait. She hadn't a telephone in her room, and the one in the hall was so public that she could never speak on it without someone loitering about, by accident or design. In front of Simon, fussing with his birds, she couldn't say, "I seem to be a prisoner. I wasn't even allowed out of the car." It seemed as if Simon were always with his birds when she was wanted on the telephone. Or Iris, with a red scarf tied attractively round her head, was dusting the banisters. Or Bella with a broom was giving her quick mouse-like skips about the hall.

But when Iris telephoned she shut herself in her room and one didn't know whom she was talking to or what she was saying. Was she now ordering the groceries or discussing the colours of paint and paper with workmen — or was she saying in a hurried whispered voice, "Have you found her yet? It's not safe for her to be wandering about. She's dangerous."

Why did she think Iris might be telephoning

about the missing woman?

At last Iris did come downstairs and a little later Antonia saw her walking in the garden with Ralph Bealey.

Now was her chance to ring Dougal. But when she hurried into the hall Simon was still there, poking his forefinger through the netting of the bird cage and making little absent clucking noises — absent because he wasn't looking at the birds but at Iris and Ralph strolling into sight. Through the open doorway in the sunshine they were like a Campbell Taylor picture, the wide light hall, the pathway running away from the open door and the two figures at the end of it.

A few minutes after that again Ralph got into his car at the gate and drove down the hillside. Iris came bustling in, saying briskly, "I must make tea. I can see the Halsteads coming. Antonia, why haven't you got your foot up?"

Then Joyce and David Halstead came in, Joyce exclaiming in her loud hearty voice, "Simon! Messing round with those birds again. But they are sweet. I'd like that yellow fellow to trim a hat. He'd look cute. I say, weren't the flowers marvellous. I just literally held my breath."

"Beautiful," Iris agreed. "I'm going to have masses of dahlias here next year. They're so colourful. That's if the wind doesn't batter them down, of course. I've got the kettle on for a cup of tea. Bella's resting, poor soul."

Joyce gave her high-pitched laugh.

"Look at Simon! I think he took me seriously when I said I'd like to trim a hat with the yellow bird."

"Oh, that's Johnnie," said Iris. "Poor Simon! He'd kill you if you harmed Johnnie. Wouldn't you, darling?"

"But that mad woman!" Joyce said suddenly. "Did you hear the broadcast? It gives me the creeps to think there's a lunatic around."

"Me, too," Iris agreed. "It quite spoilt the procession for me, thinking of her. I hope they find her before we go out tonight."

"There are a hundred and fifty thousand people in Christchurch," David Halstead pointed out reasonably. "It isn't likely we're going to be the ones to encounter this one poor old woman."

His wife shuddered.

"No, that's sense. But people like that should be shut up more safely. They shouldn't be allowed to escape."

Iris's bright restless eyes flickered round the hall.

"I quite agree," she said emphatically.

It was as they were having tea in the lounge

that the ring came at the front door, and the elderly woman with the neat grey hair, the neat black clothes and the sad blue eyes stood at the doorway.

Joyce Halstead gave a gasp and Iris sprang to her feet, the teacup clattering in its saucer.

Antonia laughed.

"Don't get so jittery, you two. It's only Bella's friend. She came the other day. I expect she's come back for her umbrella."

Iris swiftly crossed the hall to speak to the woman. Joyce sank back, looking a little shame-faced.

"They shouldn't broadcast things like that. It makes people panicky. My nerves!"

"You are being a fool," he husband told her. "What on earth would make a schizophrenic come all the way up here?"

"I know. It was silly of me. But you think those things instinctively. David, don't use those horrible words. Schizophrenic. Whatever does it mean?"

"It means someone with a split personality. They become two people, a sort of Jekyll and Hyde, I suppose."

Simon with the greatest care had put his cup and saucer on the sideboard. Now he was wiping his mouth and saying as Iris passed the door with the elderly woman, "Why, it's Miss

Rich, Bella's friend. She's been up here before. Miss Rich. That's what her name is."

"She lost her sister recently," Antonia added.

"Oh, did she? I didn't know that. But I suppose Bella wouldn't tell me. Yes, it's Miss Rich. She's perfectly harmless."

He was babbling, Antonia thought. They were all babbling. Iris came back into the room saying, "I had to wake Bella up. You remember Miss Rich, Simon. She's been here before. She's come for her umbrella. I told her a chat with Bella might do Bella good."

More babbling. What had got into everybody? Why should a schizophrenic, wandering harmlessly somewhere, upset them all so much?

Much later Iris said that Miss Rich had gone. Ralph had come home and driven her down the hill to catch her tram. Iris had a gold taffeta evening dress over her arm and was taking it to the kitchen to press it.

"Get out your dress, Antonia, and I'll press it for you," she offered.

"There's no need. I can do it."

"You'll do nothing of the kind. You'll keep off your ankle as much as possible. Because you must be able to dance tonight. It's going to be fun."

Was this a time to be having fun? She had

never felt less like dancing. She thought of Ralph Bealey's cool smooth hands on her back, of his peculiar cream-coloured face close to hers and had a moment of shuddering revulsion. But there was no use in arguing just now. She would get her dress and let Iris press it. Something would happen later. She felt that with certainty.

When she reached her room she knew that something had happened. At first it wasn't particularly obvious. The pillows on the bed were slightly crooked, the wardrobe door was open an inch. But she had made the bed in a hurry that morning and she could easily have left the door that way herself.

Then she noticed a drawer of her dresser half open and its contents rumpled as if someone had been searching for something. There was powder spilt on the dressing-table, too, an irregular pale pink trail of it.

At first it was as if she were back in the hotel room in Auckland demanding to know who had gone through her luggage. Then she was remembering vividly the way she and Bella had found Iris's room the other day, with the scrawling scarlet writing on the wall and powder spilt everywhere.

Gussie! she thought. Then he must have come back.

Almost in a dream she heard Gussie's shrill reiterated denial in her mind. "But I didn't do it! I didn't do it!" The voice on the telephone, the lighted window, the seaweed on the stairs, someone calling and crying in the night.... Supposing after all it hadn't been Gussie who had written on Iris's wall....

With that queer cold fear of the unknown rising in her again Antonia ran to the head of the stairs, calling, "Iris! Iris!"

It seemed as if everyone appeared to look up at her, but it was Iris who came up the stairs, her face full of anxiety.

"What is it, darling? Simon, switch off the iron for me, please. What's the matter, Antonia?"

Antonia was beginning to regret her momentary lack of self-control.

"Someone's been messing round in my room," she said. "It looks just like Gussie."

"It can't be Gussie!" Iris stopped dead. It was as if someone had taken her by the shoulders and pinned her where she stood.

"Well, come and see," Antonia urged.

Iris came up the stairs two at a time. She hurried into the room and stopped short, her face growing rueful.

"Oh, Tonia, I'm sorry! I didn't know I'd spilt your face powder."

"You!" Antonia exclaimed.

"Yes, and I didn't mean you to know I'd been in here, but something happened and I was called away. Oh, dear, look at the mess."

"You've done this!" Antonia repeated in indignant astonishment. "What do you think you've been up to?"

"Now, darling, don't get upset. It's those wretched missing sleeping tablets. Ralph said I've to find them. It's too dangerous to leave them about."

Antonia was aware of Iris coming close to her, her narrow pointed face, her bright eyes, like a cat's, like Ptolemy's, full of excited anticipation as he watched the flitting birds.

It was for these curious little events that she was staying, she told herself desperately. She mustn't get frightened, mustn't let that creeping horror overtake her. Iris's actions might have been completely honest and in good faith. Why should she have the feeling that the room had been deliberately left in this mess so as to entirely demoralise her? Or so as to provide evidence for other eyes — when evidence was required.

"I told you I didn't take those sleeping tablets," she said coldly. "Don't you believe me?"

Iris gave an uncomfortable laugh. Her eyes were distressed.

"I know you think that, dear, but just to be sure Ralph said—"

"And did you find them?"

"No, darling. If only you'd try to remember—"

Colour rose in Antonia's cheeks. She could no longer keep her good manners.

"You may mean it for the best, Iris, but I think you're behaving quite unforgivably. I don't know what you're up to, but make no mistake, I'll find out before I leave this house."

Iris flung out her hands.

"There you are! You see you are unbalanced, imagining I'm up to something when all I'm trying to do, as anyone can see, is to look after you. That's where you're being so *fantastic!*"

Antonia stared at her in angry exasperation. She no longer had words to express herself. She was suddenly aware of Simon at the door saying, "Come along, Iris, give it a rest."

Iris flashed round at him. Then she controlled her sharp temper and said in an injured voice, "Here I am, doing my best to look after Antonia and I get misjudged like this. I did say I was sorry, didn't I? I'll get a duster and clean up that mess."

Had she been foolish to make an issue of it, Antonia wondered. But they were attaching importance to it, too, Simon with his rough almost frightened voice, and Iris rueful, penitent, now over-anxious to please.

"It's all right. I'll do it myself," she said slowly. "I just don't care to have my things interfered with, that's all."

"Of course not. Simon, don't look so angry with me. I was looking for those missing sleeping tablets," she heard Iris explaining as she and Simon went away.

Melodrama, that's what it was. Henrietta would love it. She suddenly wanted to laugh, and pressed her hand over her mouth, staring at the carelessly spilt face powder. But was it carelessly spilt? It looked as if someone had dipped a finger in it and tried to form clumsy letters. What did they look like? An I and an A, then a blur, then very distinctly another A. No, the first letter might have been meant to be an L, not an I. An L and an A, and yes, that was an R and another A. The name came flashing into Antonia's head. *Laura!*

Her brain whirling, Antonia crossed to the window, instinctively throwing it open to get some fresh air. As she did so she saw a man's head appear over the low stone fence that ran round the cliff's edge, screening the steep dangerous drop to the sea. Putting his hands on the parapet the man sprang over lightly and with a quick look up at the house began walking across the lawn. It was Dougal Conroy.

She waved to him wildly. "Dougal! Dougal! Wait there. I'm coming down to see you."

He lifted his head. It seemed, even from that distance, as if his face lighted up. He pointed to something and she realised with amusement that he meant her to come down the fire escape which ran down from her window. Did he think she was locked in her room?

But it would be a good idea. The lounge didn't overlook this part of the garden. She might be able to talk to Dougal unobserved.

She thrust her legs over the window sill and began to descend the steep ladder.

Dougal was at the bottom when she slid off the last step. Without saying anything at all he took her in his arms.

Then, for a minute, it was as if nothing else had ever happened. This was where the world began. How funny, how very funny and precious it was that Dougal Conroy with his serious face, his blue earnest eyes, his golden brows, his stiff untidy hair, had this magic.

All at once he let her go and said in embarrassment, "I'm sorry. I didn't mean to do that."

"Dougal Conroy, if you say you're sorry for that I'll just quietly push you over that cliff."

He took a step away. There were grim lines in his cheeks.

"Don't say that," he said, "because I think someone has been pushed over."

And the thick cloud of horror was back, pressing on her, blotting out the bright day.

"Gussie!" she whispered. "Not Gussie."

"I don't know. I went down on a rope. I tied it to the parapet. I took the opportunity while everyone was away."

"Yes?"

She tried not to think of him hanging over that dangerous drop. She listened with an increasing sense of apprehension as he said, "There's a small bush half torn out about twenty feet down. This was caught on it." He showed her a fragment of faded blue cotton material. She had a sudden vivid memory of Gussie's thin brown body in a torn shirt and patched trousers, Gussie, thin, sly, furtive, untruthful, but alive, blessedly alive.

"But the fishing lines, Dougal," she got out at last.

"They could have been planted, couldn't they?"

She nodded miserably.

"I suppose so. But that bit of stuff — it isn't conclusive proof. It could be a bit of Bella's washing, torn in the wind. It's awfully windy up here."

Dougal looked at her unbelievingly.

"Then if that is what happened to Gussie,"

she said slowly, unwillingly, "it's because of something that he knew or something he had, something that was dangerous. Dougal, we have to find out what it was."

"Yes, I see that."

"Listen," she said eagerly, "don't tell the police yet what you've found. If they arrive it will put everyone too much on their guard and we might find out nothing. I have a better plan. We're all supposed to be going to the dance tonight. I'll go, but in an hour or so I'll slip out and get a taxi and come back. You meet me here at eleven o'clock. Bella by then, if my guess is right, will be drunk and we'll have the place to ourselves."

"I say! Well, I say!" Suddenly there came the loud voice of Joyce Halstead. "Look at those two lovebirds!"

She had come round the house with her husband and now was laughing and saying, "It's all right, we won't disturb you. But that's a chilly spot, isn't it?"

"All right?" Antonia said softly to Dougal, at the same time smiling at Joyce and waving her away.

"All right," he agreed. "But I wish you didn't need to go to the dance."

"I must. They'd never leave me here alone. Not now."

"No, I suppose not. But I hate you going with them the way things are. I hate leaving you here."

"Why, Dougal!" – she tried to be facetious, but her unsteady voice betrayed her – "you couldn't be a little bit in love with me? Not with my hair this colour. You don't like this colour. You have a thing about it."

"In love with you!" he exclaimed despairingly. "How the devil can I be? With all that money!"

"Money!" she repeated. "You mean Aunt Laura's legacy? But surely you have a false idea of the value of four thousand pounds. Or in New Zealand is it worth more–" She stopped suddenly, reading his anguished expression. "Dougal there's more!" she whispered. "That's what you thought I ought to know?"

He nodded.

"Then tell me quickly."

"I should say there's more," he answered with the deepest gloom. "Only about four hundred thousand pounds more."

# XVIII

Simon was alone in the hall when she went in. He had the lemon-coloured bird, Johnnie, on his finger, and he was cautiously lifting it to his lips and making soft kissing sounds. The bird, after regarding Simon intently with its pin-head bright eyes, suddenly rubbed its tiny hooked beak against Simon's lips and whispered and twittered ecstatically.

At the sound of Antonia's footsteps Simon turned his head carefully.

"Did you close the door?" he whispered.

"Yes."

"I've shut Ptolemy in the woodshed. Iris would be furious if she knew." He rubbed his thick gentle finger down the bird's sleek back. "I've got to have some time with Johnnie. He's forgetting his vocabulary. He's nervous, too."

At that moment he heard Iris coming from

the kitchen and he swiftly opened the cage door and slipped the bird inside. It wasn't only Johnnie who was nervous, Antonia reflected. Simon himself was acting like a child stealing jam. He would have to stand up for his rights more than this if he were going to be happy with Iris. Would he ever dare to?

Iris glanced at them and went on.

Simon, watching her retreat, said in a low voice, "I say, Tonia, don't hold it against Iris that she looked for those sleeping pills. She'd mean it for the best."

But the missing sleeping pills and her disturbed room had shrunk into insignificance in view of what she had just heard.

"Oh, that," said Antonia vaguely. "Oh, look! Miss Rich has forgotten her umbrella again."

She pointed to it still standing in the hall stand. Simon gave an exclamation. Then he began fussing like an old woman, "Oh, dear! How unfortunate! It's because it's not raining, of course. She wouldn't think of it."

"She can't want it very much," Antonia said lightly. "If you ask me she isn't quite right here." She pointed to her head, smiling at Simon, thinking what an old woman he was in some ways, with his fussing over things. How would he act if it had been he to whom Aunt Laura had left all that money?

She went upstairs to have a bath and dress in her evening clothes. How could she be expected to concentrate on missing sleeping tablets or even that tremendous fortune when she had just discovered that Dougal Conroy was in love with her. How could she possibly be interested in sleeping tablets now when she never wanted to sleep a minute that she could be awake thinking of Dougal with his golden brows, his funny serious eyes, and his illuminating smile.

She wanted to ring Henrietta and say, "I've converted your son. I've converted him to red hair!"

But being an heiress was going to be an awful bother. Just fancy old Aunt Laura having all that money. One had always known Uncle Joe had been wealthy, but he had died twenty-five years ago and Aunt Laura could so easily have dissipated all his fortune in her eternal travelling. Apparently she had been extremely careful of it. Probably she had made good investments and added to it. Poor Aunt Laura, anchored at last, unwillingly, with withered flowers on her grave.

That queer scratching in the spilt powder on her dressing-table... It was growing dark. Antonia switched on the light to look at the writing again. But now it didn't look like anything, just vague marks in pale pink dust. Had she imagined the letters? Probably, in her agitated state of mind, she had.

She got a duster and vigorously brushed away the powder. Tonight she and Dougal were going to find out something much more definite than faint hieroglyphics made with cosmetics. The thought of Gussie crossed her mind and suddenly she was shivering uncontrollably.

Dougal! she thought, desperately conjuring up his face in her mind, his gentle eyes, the slight entrancing roughness of his skin, his lips soft and yet hard on hers.

"You're my star now," she murmured. "Stay with me." And the image of Gussie's skinny terrified body being swallowed in the moonlit sea faded and she began to hum resolutely to herself as she brushed her hair and saw the amber lights starting in it.

They were all to dress for the dance before dinner, Iris had said. The next three hours were simply a space of time that had to be lived through before somehow she got back to the Hilltop and met Dougal and they made their search for whatever it was that Gussie had hidden.

(Gussie with seaweed in his hair and little fishes swimming about his unaware fingers.)

She stayed upstairs until the last possible minute, and when she went down everyone was waiting for dinner.

Joyce Halstead in a bright red velvet dress that made her look like a piece of plush furniture in an opera house cried, "Ah ha! I know now who the light in Antonia's eye is for!"

"Oh!" said Simon heartily. "Who's that?"

"Why, Dougal Conroy, of course. I caught them. Antonia, you don't mind me telling?"

Iris handed Antonia a glass of sherry.

"Antonia!" she said delightedly. "Is Dougal in love with you?"

"I wouldn't think so. He's too wise. You see," she said clearly, "he isn't a fortune hunter."

"Good gracious, have you a lot of money?" Joyce asked inquisitively.

"I didn't know I had, but it seems I have. Or will have next month when I'm twenty-four. It's a legacy from my aunt," she explained to the Halsteads. "Nearly a half a million. It sounds an awful lot, doesn't it. Quite frankly it terrifies me."

"Gosh!" breathed Joyce.

"Antonia, you weren't supposed to know that," Simon said heavily.

"Is that what Dougal Conroy was talking to you about?" said Iris. "I don't think that's very ethical. Do you, Simon? In view of the instructions in the will."

"You see," Antonia said, still talking to the

Halsteads, "my dear old Aunt Laura had a funny idea that if I didn't know I was an heiress I would be protected from fortune hunters. But what she didn't realise was that other people would have ways of finding out and that *I* would be the only person in the dark. Which is a little inconvenient and confusing."

Ralph Bealey spoke for the first time.

"Aren't you rather jumping to conclusions about people's motives?" He was twisting his sherry glass in his long thin fingers. In her excited imagination his face seemed distorted, his nose too crooked, his eyes extraordinarily close-set, his mouth a straight flat scar.

"I wouldn't think so," she answered lightly. "Money's a wonderful comfort to some people. Personally, I think it's an awful nuisance. I long to be loved for myself alone."

"Don't be childish," said Iris. "Whoever found money a nuisance? Simon, do for goodness' sake fill people's glasses. As a barman you're hopeless." She picked up the sherry bottle. Her little shoulders above her gold dress were white and smooth, small as a child's, her hair woven in a rope round her head had its enchanting pussy willow silver. She looked made for caresses and gentleness until you saw her narrow white wary face and her eyes bright with intelligence.

It was easy to see that she didn't care for the conversation. Simon didn't care for it either. He swallowed his sherry in one gulp and his face seemed to grow red and hot all at once.

"I'll speak to Conroy tomorrow," Antonia heard him saying to Iris as he took the sherry bottle from her.

"Oh, if Antonia knows it's too late," Iris said lightly. "Anyway, she soon would have had to know. But it was to be such a marvellous birthday surprise. The way Simon and I have been keeping that secret!"

"And supposing," said David Halstead in his serious considering way, "Antonia shouldn't live to inherit the capital—"

"Supposing you can't hang out another month," Joyce finished gaily, "who gets all this wealth?"

But before anyone could answer that question there was a sudden commotion in the hall. Simon's birds were twittering in an ecstasy of fear. The wires of the cage were thrumming. One bird's voice was raised above the rest in a pitiful squawking.

Simon reached the door first, but everyone was in time to see the white cat streak across the hall with the little yellow bird in its mouth.

The wires of the cage had broken at one end and through the narrow aperture, as Johnnie sat preening himself on his perch, Ptolemy must have stolen a stealthy paw.

With a cry of anguish Simon gave chase.

Joyce Halstead, inevitably, was the first to speak.

"My, it's the yellow one, too! Simon's nuts about him, isn't he?"

"That's putting it mildly," Iris said ruefully. She tried to twist the broken wires of the cage. The birds within flew about agitatedly, like scraps of pastel-coloured silk, opening their tiny parakeet beaks and twittering in their hoarse shrill voices. "Anyway," she couldn't help adding, with a note of pride in her voice, "Ptolemy's a good cat. A good cat always gets its prey."

As she spoke Simon came back into the hall. He had the yellow bird in his hand. It lay limply, its beak opening and shutting. Two of Simon's fingers were bleeding where Ptolemy had scratched him.

"Simon, I'm sorry," Iris said.

He held the bird out to her. His small blue eyes were full of angry despair.

"Look what your cat's done! Look!"

Iris went to him. "Well, darling, I can't help it. I can't change a cat's nature, can I? I've said I'm sorry and I really am. But after all it's only one little bird. It's not the end of the world."

She tucked her hand in his arm and gave him a little appealing hug. "For heaven's sake, don't be so sentimental."

Simon gave her one bewildered accusing look. Then he shook her off, drew the bird close to his breast and without another word went upstairs.

Iris watched him out of sight. She flung out her hands.

"Isn't he a great baby! Well, we're not going to let that spoil our evening. Ralph, or David, do you think you could make the cage secure before there's another tragedy? And then if Simon doesn't come down we'll start dinner without him."

Simon didn't come down to dinner. It was an uncomfortable meal with everyone trying to be normal. It was so easy to know what they were all thinking. This is an unlucky house. First a boy, a little brat, but a human being none the less, goes missing, and now Simon's favourite bird dies. What will be next?

There was only one cheerful note about it, and that was that Bella's face had its dim brightness again. Gussie still hadn't appeared, it was true, and it seemed almost inevitable that he was drowned, but arrangements had at last been made for her sick husband to come up to the Hilltop. She was full of gratitude to Iris who, it appeared, had made strenuous efforts to get permission for him to leave the hospital at once.

Iris herself was reticent about it.

"He can't live long, poor devil, and it means Bella has to nurse him. But if they can have this bit of time together it's only right they should. One has to be human."

Joyce and David Halstead nodded in sympathetic agreement, full of admiration for Iris's thoughtfulness. Antonia would have been full of admiration, too, if she hadn't known about the scrap of blue cotton caught on a bush halfway down the sheer drop of a cliff, and if she had been able to stop thinking about Simon grieving over the dying bird.

It was clear that Bella loved her husband a great deal more than she had loved her difficult son. Now, at least, she had one source of happiness. Even if, in some strange way, it were a bribe. . . .

Simon came down with Iris when they were ready to leave for town. His eyes were puffy as if he had been crying. Iris held his arm affectionately.

"We're all ready," she said gaily. "Let's have one more drink before we go. Some along, Simon. Drown your sorrows."

"Is Johnnie dead?" Antonia asked Simon softly.

He looked at her with his swollen eyes. Then he said, "What do you think?" He began to laugh in a loud belligerent way. "Joyce will have the ornament for her hat after all. Isn't that a joke? Eh? Isn't that a joke!"

# XIX

As soon as she met him in the glimmer of moonlight at the gate Dougal said to her, "How did you get away?"

Antonia laughed. She had on a dress of some light material that gleamed in the dark and made her look not quite real, like thistledown or sea spray. She didn't look as if she remotely had any connection with suspicious happenings, much less murder. He wanted to kiss her again, but he had himself well in hand now. Antonia Webb, with her ensnaring red hair, her courage and her forbidding fortune was not for him. He must find his quiet-voiced girl for whom he could toil happily all his life. Antonia must take her money and go away safely. She must be no more than a dream.

But he longed now to touch her. He had to clench his fingers in his palms.

"Oh, I got away very simply," she said. "I told them my ankle was hurting – and so it was – and I wanted to put it up for a while. Iris came with me to the cloakroom, but she left me, thank goodness, and I just slipped out the back way and got a taxi."

She had a flower in her hair, Dougal noticed. It was so incongruous that she should be here searching for evidence of a murder dressed like that with a flower in her hair.

"There were flowers everywhere," she was saying. "They were beautiful. But I had the queer feeling all the time that everything was poisonous. I think they wanted me to go to-night to get a little drunk, then it would be so much easier to give me the sleeping tablets, the ones they've carefully hidden to make it look as if I've got them and mean to take them at the first opportunity. Last night was just a rehearsal – you know, I'm a little sorry for Joyce and David who are so obviously wanted as witnesses, genuine ones. They're just the type, a little stupid, gullible, easily flattered. And Ralph Bealey's so useful as a doctor on the scene."

"Stop that now! That's not going to happen!" Dougal said harshly.

"Dougal, it's Simon who gets all the money if I don't come of age, isn't it?" she asked.

He could hardly bear her reflective detached voice, speaking so calmly about what might so easily have happened.

All he could say was, "Yes. Simon gets it."

"Simon!" she echoed sadly. "And yet he cried over a dead bird." She slipped her arm in his. "Well, come on, we must hurry. Dougal you're shaking."

"I'm cold. I've been waiting here a while." He wasn't cold at all, although the wind off the sea was reaching over the top of the hill and swooping down to whisper silkily in the tussocks. The big white house, stark against the moonlit sky, was a hostile place now. After tonight, he thought, they would never go in it again. Just this last thing had to be found, the connecting link between Gussie's disappearance and the things that had happened to Antonia. But in spite of that having to be done he wanted to pick her up in his arms and carry her out to his car and put her in it and drive away from this mysterious menacing place for ever.

It was useless, however, to try to persuade Antonia to have no part in the discovery that had to be made. Anyway, there could be no danger for a little time with only Bella in the house and she probably provided with a new bottle of brandy.

"Let's get this over," he said. "But the moment we find anything incriminating we go for the police. Promise."

"All right," she promised gaily. "It can be their show then and welcome. Let's find Bella first."

As they had expected, Bella was in the kitchen. She came to the door in swift alarm at the sound of their footsteps. There was no sign of the brandy bottle, but there was an empty glass on the table and Bella's cheeks were suspiciously flushed and her eyes glazed.

"Miss Webb!" she exclaimed. "Mr. Conroy! Why aren't you at the dance?"

"Bella," said Antonia seriously, "we want to find something Gussie had. We're going to search his room."

Bella took a step back. Her face grew wary.

"What do you suppose he had?"

"That's what we don't know. But it's important. It will lead us to finding out what's happened to him."

Bella's eyes filled with tears.

"It's too late for that. He's dead. Drowned. The police say there's not much hope at this stage. I've got to tell Jim tomorrow. We were always afraid Gussie'd come to a bad end. Perhaps it's for the best, before he did worse things. That's the only way to look at it."

The brandy was making Bella gloomily philosophical. Dougal said firmly, "I'm sorry Bella, but whether you let us or not we're going to search Gussie's room. If we don't the police will."

"The police!" Now the fear was back in her eyes, the wary apprehension that one could startle there at almost any time.

"I'm afraid so. Show us the way, will you?"

Wordlessly Bella indicated a door leading from the passage opposite. Then she began to sob, biting her knuckles fiercely to control herself.

There was no time now for sympathy. Antonia was first in the little room and had switched on the light which showed the bare interior, the narrow bed, the chest of drawers, a chair, a shabby wool rug, and in the corner a jar of greenish water in which a couple of tadpoles moved torpidly. Their mute witness to Gussie's recent existence was the most pathetic of all. Antonia hung over them a minute, but Dougal began a systematic search, pulling open drawers and lifting the mattress and blankets off the bed.

There was nothing strange or out of the way here, only a boy's scanty treasures, a broken pocket knife, a round white pebble from the beach, a selection of fish hooks, the sick forgotten tadpoles in the slimy water.

"It's extraordinarily difficult to find something when one doesn't know what one's looking for," Antonia murmured. "If an old woman gave it to him I should think it would be a ring, or a—" She stopped short as a faint crying sound reached their ears.

Was it a cry? It had come and drifted away, a wisp of sound, perhaps the wind, perhaps a passing seabird.

Antonia stood rigid.

"Dougal! Listen!"

Was it a human cry? It came again, fainter, infinitely mournful, the ghost of a cry, the voice of someone who had given up hope.

Quick as a flash Antonia had darted out of the room.

Dougal went to follow her, but in the passage Bella clutched at his arm. She had something in her hand.

"I wonder if this is what you're looking for," she said in a breathless whisper. "It might be. Mark you, I'm only giving it to you because Miss Webb was good to Gussie. She was the only one who was good to him." Bella's voice died away brokenly.

Without looking at the flat article, thrusting it into his pocket, Dougal made to go in pursuit of Antonia. But once more Bella stopped him.

"No," she said. "Not that way. This way."

"But I must go with Antonia."

"She'll come back when she doesn't find anything. Come and I'll show you."

Hurrying ahead of him, a little unsteady, a quaint little tipsy mouse, Bella led him to the cellar stairs. As she went down them and fumbled with the lock of the door at the bottom a wail, so close that it was like a cold breath on Dougal's cheek, sounded.

"Now, now," said Bella irritably. "Stop that, will you. We don't want that all night."

She opened the door, revealing the dimly-lit interior.

"There's who you want, I think," she said breathlessly. "And I'm only showing you because I'm worried about her. They said she was gone for good and now she's back and I don't like it. Someone ought to be told about it." She clutched Dougal's arm a minute, peering into his face with her small poignant eyes. "But don't say it was me showed you!" she begged. Then as if she heard something she drew in her breath sharply and scuttered past him up the stairs.

Dougal stepped into the cold room lit only by a guttering candle, and saw the shadowy little creature in the corner crouched on the end of a camp bed, the only article of furniture in the room.

"Who the devil are you?" he asked, startled.

The woman raised her face. In the dim light he could see the shine of tears on her cheeks.

"And that will be all you need to know, Mr. Interfering Conroy!" came a thick voice behind him.

The blow came before he could even turn his head.

There was only one thought in Antonia's mind — the room in the empty wing from where, once before, the sound of crying had come. Lifting her long skirts she ran up the uncarpeted stairs and along the corridor to the third room. She didn't look to see if Dougal were following. She hadn't time to tell him of her intuition. The thing to do was to get there before the door was locked, before the light was switched off, and to see who was there crying for help, or for mere loneliness and sorrow.

The door wasn't locked. It opened when she turned the knob. The room was in darkness save for a faint glimmer from the window.

"Is anyone there?" Antonia whispered. She thought she heard someone move, a stealthy movement in the darkness. Her heart was pounding. She fumbled for the light switch, found it and switched the light on.

The room was quite empty.

Dust still lay on the floor and round the ledges. There were faint imprints in the dust on the floor, but they could have been made by anyone in the last few days. There were marks on the mantelpiece, too, as if someone had dragged a finger through the dust. But wait! Were they those queer hieroglyphics again? There seemed to be the rough shape of the letter M.

Antonia stared at them thoughtfully. She scarcely heard the door shut. It was more instinct than sound that made her turn.

How could the door have shut so neatly and silently? If the wind had blown it it would have banged. Her heart pounding again, she took half a dozen quick steps across the room to open the door. The knob turned in her hand but the door wouldn't open. It was locked!

Panic filled her. She rattled the knob, calling, "Open the door! Whoever's there, open the door and don't be silly! This is no joke."

There was no sound.

When once before the door had been locked it had been from the inside, and she had been free to go away, puzzled and frightened, to be sure, but free. Now she was the one on the inside. She was the prisoner.

She began to bang on the panels.

"For heaven's sake, who's playing this stupid joke on me! *Please* open the door!"

Then there was a sound from the other side. There was a faint breathy laugh. And the voice that had spoken to her on the telephone in Auckland, the slow thick whispering voice, said, "Just have a little patience, Antonia, dear. It's your turn presently."

After that, stealthy footsteps went away down the corridor. She was left clinging to the door, sick with fear, afraid even to call for help.

When at last she could bring herself to move she crossed to the window and tried to open it. The frame had jammed, probably from long disuse, and she couldn't force it up more than an inch or two. In any case that was of no help for she knew there was a long drop to the ground, with no convenient fire escape here. There was no escape that way – unless a leap through broken glass was preferable to what was going to happen in here.

Whose had been that voice? The only man she knew to be in the house at present was Dougal. Surely it couldn't have been Dougal. Simon or Ralph Bealey or even innocent-looking David Halstead could have followed her here half an hour ago. Or it could even have been some complete stranger.

Whoever it was, it was like her nightmare

of the other night in reality, the thick voice saying, "It's your turn next," and the hands approaching. . .

In her thin evening dress she was shivering violently. The most dreadful thing of all was that she was afraid to call out again. She remembered that other voice crying and the battering on the window, and she wondered if someone had been threatening that person into an ecstasy of terror. Presently, would she begin battering on the window. . .

Dougal, where are you? Why didn't you follow me? Dougal, what's happened? Are you hurt, or— But she couldn't go on with her inward cry. It *couldn't* be Dougal!

Crouched against the wall in the horrible dusty room she suddenly became rigid again.

For the other voice had recommenced calling. Somewhere below her, far off, but quite distinct, came the high unhappy sound. And now it seemed to be articulate.

"Where's Laura?" it was crying. "Laura! Save Laura! Save poor Laura!"

In a little interval of silence Antonia heard Iris's white cat mewing in the garden, a thin bodiless sound not remotely resembling the scream it had given the other night. Or was it really Ptolemy who had screamed. . . "A good cat always gets its prey," Iris had said in her smug callous voice. Was she the cat's prey? But who was the cat? Who was the cat?

"Lau-ra..." came the forlorn voice, and Antonia, her fingers thrust into her ears, began to sob in great breathless gasps.

# XX

Henrietta had talked of little else but the mysterious disappearance of Gussie since it had happened. She had given Dougal no peace.

"Take my word for it, that boy wouldn't be washed off a rock. He's like a limpet."

But Dougal was more disappointingly reticent than ever, and Ethel had nothing to contribute to the drama beyond exclamations of horror and a giggle that was more high-pitched and convulsive than before. When Miss Fox arrived unexpectedly that evening Henrietta recognised a kindred spirit and welcomed her ardently.

They were completely opposite in appearance. Henrietta made Miss Fox think of a large jar packed and overflowing with brightly hued flowers, diffusing their perfume and their untidy petals and their colours everywhere. Miss

Fox herself was immaculately neat, flat as a piece of plywood, sharp-faced and caustic. But their minds worked the same way. They both had an instinct for the dramatic.

Over a glass of sherry Miss Fox confided her reason for coming.

"It's really Mr. Conroy I wanted to see. There's something he ought to know."

"Oh, Dougal's disappeared," Henrietta said. "He just comes and goes these days. Never says a word. It's most exasperating. But he's up to something. He just wasn't with us at dinner tonight, I mean mentally, and now he's gone off somewhere again. It's useless to look for Gussie, of course. It might be weeks before his body's washed up. If only that nice girl Antonia is all right. You know she fell down the stairs, don't you? Slipped on seaweed! Now seaweed doesn't walk into a house. It must have been put on the stairs intentionally. If you ask me, it's all part of a diabolical plot."

Miss Fox clasped her bony hands in a state of extreme tension.

"But this is the question, Mrs. Conroy. Where is Laura Mildmay's companion?"

"Companion! What's this?" Henrietta leaned forward eagerly. "Has someone else disappeared?"

Miss Fox nodded, her thin nostrils quivering.

"It's those people who knew Iris Matthews —
or Mrs. Simon Mildmay now — on the ship.
They remembered something that they thought
we ought to know. Iris was a stewardess, you
see, and she was looking after these two women
who were both quite ill."

"Iris a stewardess! Does Dougal know this?
Oh, *why* does he insist on keeping me in the
dark! This may be vital information. And after
me specially writing that letter, too."

Miss Fox was startled.

"That anonymous letter, Mrs. Conroy? Did
you write it?"

"None but I," Henrietta admitted with satisfaction. "I said right from the start that Iris's
antecedents should be looked into, but as you
could expect, my clever son would take no
notice of his mother. So I thought I'd see what
notice he would take of a stranger. You did
act on that letter, Miss Fox?"

"I thought it wise to make enquiries — in
view of the size of the Mildmay estate, of
course."

Henrietta nodded eagerly.

"And you found that Miss Matthews occu-
pied the humble position of stewardess on a
ship, Miss Iris with all her airs! Now we're
getting somewhere. But tell me, who was the
other woman? You said there were two."

"The other one was Miss Mildmay's companion, a Miss Rich. Apparently they'd travelled together for years and were inseparable. She must have been in Auckland with them when Miss Mildmay was dying, but what has happened to her since? Tell me that."

Miss Fox's sharp eyes glinted triumphantly. For once Henrietta was speechless, shaking her head in a puzzled manner.

Miss Fox went on, "When I heard that broadcast today for a missing woman I don't know why it was that I said to myself. 'This is something that should be enquired into.' Now why should I have the hunch that that missing woman, feeble-minded, poor soul, and probably with no memory, was Laura Mildmay's companion, Miss Rich?"

"I can't imagine!" Henrietta murmured. Then she sprang up, trembling with excitement. "I have it! The light in the window! The mysterious light in the empty wing at the Hilltop! They've had her up there. And it's she who's been doing these things to Antonia, because in her dim-witted way she's jealous. Antonia's alive, Laura's dead. Or perhaps she's just the kind of mental patient who is dangerous. I see it all now!"

Miss Fox was becoming infected with Henrietta's excitement.

"But why should they hide her like that?"

"Well, it's unpleasant having a lunatic in the house. Perhaps they thought it would frighten Antonia. They found some people to look after her and thought it wisest just to say nothing."

"It all sounds very plausible," Miss Fox said reflectively, "but we may be guessing quite wrong. This missing woman may have no connection at all with the Hilltop."

Henrietta waved that aside.

"Now don't you have Dougal's passion for evidence! Some cases have to worked out by intuition alone. Look, come and I'll show you the window where the light used to be. I thought at first it was burglars." Talking all the time, she drew back the window curtains to look up the hillside.

Then she gave a great gasp. Her big soft hand clenched on Miss Fox's narrow shoulder.

"Look at that!" she whispered. "The light's on in the third window again!"

A few minutes later Ethel was summoned from the kitchen. When she saw Henrietta pointing a shotgun at her she gave a high-pitched scream.

Henrietta changed the direction of the gun apologetically.

"Sorry, Ethel! This wasn't meant to be pointed at you. I'm not threatening you or anything.

It's loaded, I know. I've always insisted on having a loaded gun in the house since my husband died. I've never shot in my life, but I swear I could if I tried."

Ethel gasped speechlessly.

"Get your coat on," said Henrietta briskly. "We're going up to Hilltop. I'm taking the gun in case we encounter violence. We must be prepared."

Ethel's plump face paled. She looked on the verge of begging to be left out of this adventure. But obedience to Henrietta's dominant personality won. She went meekly to put on her outdoor shoes, and Henrietta, flinging on her own coat, her big face shining with excitement, shouted, "Come on, the three musketeers! Action at last!"

It was Miss Fox who remained practical.

"But what are we going to do when we get there? We can't just demand to see what's in that room. They'll probably make us wait and in the meantime shift whoever's in there."

Henrietta reflected. "You're quite right." She began to laugh in hearty merriment. "And I can hardly appear at the front door with a shotgun in my hand, can I? Obviously we have to do things by stealth. There's only one way."

Miss Fox, her eyes snapping, hung on Henrietta's words.

"We can look through the window," Henrietta pronounced dramatically.

Ethel, who had just returned to the room, gave a small squeal.

"But the window must be thirty feet from the ground," Miss Fox protested.

"Exactly. Therefore we take a ladder. Now, Ethel, don't look so dazed. Go and unlock the toolshed. Surely three women can carry a ladder up a hill. And hurry before Dougal comes and spoils our fun."

# XXI

The footsteps were coming back along the passage. Antonia could neither move nor make a sound. She watched in an agony of fear as the doorknob turned and slowly the door began to open.

Then a familiar voice came and in her enormous relief her fear vanished.

"Well, Antonia, are you a little nervous now? Just a little nervous?"

She was so intensely thankful that it wasn't Dougal. If fantastically, it had been Dougal she would have begged to die at once.

She looked levelly into Ralph Bealey's cream-coloured face with the narrowed glinting eyes.

"I'm not nervous at all. I just think you're behaving in an extraordinarily silly way. You can't imagine I won't tell Iris and Simon."

He gave his flat smile which was no more

than a baring of his teeth.

"If you're able to, my dear. And if they care to listen, of course. I rather fancy they won't be particularly interested." He closed the door behind him and took a step towards her. There was a red carnation in his buttonhole. His evening clothes became his slim body very well. His narrow face with its close-set vicious eyes had an almost macabre look above his conventional clothing. A death's head, Antonia thought tritely. It was extraordinary how, now that she knew her enemy, she was no longer afraid.

"You're a bit of a Bluebeard, aren't you," she said, "locking up women like this. Who is it downstairs who keeps calling Laura? Is she locked up, too?"

He frowned. She sensed that he would have liked her to be petrified with terror. He was a sadist, of course, as well as— A tremor passed through her. Was he a murderer? Or about to be one?

"The identity of that person," he said, "can no longer interest you." Suddenly he made a movement towards her. "You're very lovely. Killing you is the last thing I want to do. Why don't you do as I asked?"

"As you asked?" Antonia queried coldly.

"Marry me."

She gave an incredulous laugh.

"What an extraordinary sense of humour you have. No, that's too much to believe, that you could want to kill me in one minute and marry me in the next. And all for that stupid money. Either way, you get it, don't you? You share with Iris. But what hold have you over Iris? And what happens to Simon? Or is he in this comic-strip plot, too?"

His thin brows were raised in admiration.

"My God, you are too good to die! Marry me, and I swear I'll treat you right."

"And what would Iris say to that?"

"Iris?" He swore vulgarly. "She can't complain. She divorced me of her own free will."

"So that's it!" Antonia murmured. "Of course. How simple. You understand each other, you know each other's little ways. I suppose she deserted you while you were in jail."

"How did you know that?" His suavity was beginning to disappear, he was showing himself, the wary unscrupulous criminal.

"It leaps to the mind. You'd catch up on her, of course. Poor Iris, what a shock for her. But tell me one thing. Why did you go to all that trouble to search my bags in Auckland?"

He relaxed enough to give a small triumphant smile. "I got what I wanted."

Vaguely Antonia remembered that old letter

285

of Aunt Laura's torn across the bottom. That was the only thing she had been able to find missing. But what could that mean to him?"

She said with all the lightness she could assume, "If I'm to die you might as well tell me the whole story first."

As she spoke the voice from below which had been silent for some time suddenly began again. At first it was just a long drawn-out cry, then "Laura!" came the pathetic call.

Antonia saw the change come over Ralph Bealey, the drawn brows and the faint glisten on his yellowish skin. He can't stand that, she thought, and at the same time her fear returned. There would be no more bargaining, he was the criminal again, always listening, always with a time limit.

She backed away as he came towards her.

"Don't touch me!" she whispered. "Don't! I'll scream!"

"And who do you think is going to hear?"

"Dougal will hear. Dougal Conroy. He's in the house. Didn't you know? And Bella."

(But if Dougal were there, why hadn't he been looking for her by now?)

His smile with its faint snarl answered her.

"Don't waste your breath shouting. I've fixed Bella. That's why I kept you waiting. And your

286

brave little interfering pokey-nosed lawyer's dead."

She couldn't speak. She looked at him desperately, silently begging him to admit he was lying. (*But why didn't Dougal come?*)

He had taken something from his pocket. His eyes were small, vicious, terrible.

"I'm just going to give you a little injection. Oddly enough, I am a doctor, if not actually a practising one. Just this one prick and you won't know another thing."

"And neither will you, *Doctor* Bealey, if you take one more step!" came a strident triumphant voice from the window.

There was the sound of breaking glass. Then, with one tremendous heave, Henrietta had the jammed window pushed up and was stepping, breathing heavily, into the room, the absurd shotgun held in front of her.

Antonia had a crazy sensation that she was in a cinema watching an absurd impossible comedy — that wasn't a comedy at all, because behind Henrietta's joviality and triumph there was a deadly purpose, and behind Ralph Bealey's astonishment fear showed in the glisten of perspiration on his forehead, in the trapped look in his eyes, the fear of the hunted who knew what it was to be caught.

In a daze she was aware of two more forms

following Henrietta, of Miss Fox's neat nimble body slipping into the room, and of plump Ethel, giggling hysterically, in the window frame.

"Antonia, are you all right?" Henrietta demanded, still keeping the gun pointed dangerously at Ralph Bealey. "What *is* all this nonsense? We expect to find a strange woman locked up and here's this going on. Is this man threatening to kill you, Antonia?"

In words it all sounded so melodramatic and unreal. Antonia wanted to laugh, but something kept stopping her laugh, some dreadful apprehension.

"He seemed to be. He was probably bluffing."

"Not so much bluff about it," Henrietta said, determined that her dramatic appearance had been only in the nick of time. "We'll tie him up and search him. Ethel! Miss Fox! The rope. Now, Doctor Bealey, I'm scared stiff of this weapon. I've never handled one before and I expect it to go off any minute. So don't do anything to startle me. Just quietly let these ladies secure you. They'll be gentle, but firm. Ethel's very strong."

Ethel, her face now a deep maroon colour, giggled convulsively. She clambered into the room, producing from the pocket of her overcoat a length of strong cord. The muscles of her firmly-fleshed arms showed through her sleeves. There was no doubting that she was capable of doing a secure job.

It must have been the most ignominious event in the whole of Ralph Bealey's chequered career. Henrietta's gun was wavering dangerously and there was a light in her eyes that showed she was longing to press the trigger. She was saying, "If this is out of order we'll apologise sincerely. But one must play safe."

Doctor Bealey's face was a yellow mask as Miss Fox tripped briskly about him and Ethel breathed down his neck. Antonia again wanted to laugh to relieve the awful tension, but she couldn't, her laughter was throttled. There was only one thing she had to do. It was to find Dougal's body.

At first her legs were not going to support her. Then, by sheer effort of will, she got out of the room and down the stairs.

Dougal was seated on the bottom step, his head in his hands, his hair ruffled over his forehead. On the back of his head there was a swelling and some blood.

Antonia fell on her knees beside him, giving a little croon of joy.

"Oh Dougal, you're not dead! He said you were dead! I knew he was lying. Oh, my darling!"

Dougal jerked his head up, looking at her

with anguished eyes. All his healthy colour had drained away.

"Wouldn't you know this would happen to me!" he said in a faint disgusted voice. "Just when you need me. I didn't even see who knocked me on the head. I've been trying to get to you. But the damn floor keeps hitting me."

"Dougal, your poor head! But you're alive! Thank God you're alive!"

She was aware of tears running down her cheeks and of him looking at her in puzzled wonder and anger.

"I might as well be dead. I'm so damned futile. Darling, don't cry."

A heavy footstep sounded. A shadow fell across them. Antonia looked up. It was Simon.

It was Simon, and yet the face was no longer Simon's affable rather vacuous one. There were deep lines in it, the little puffy eyes were hard as stones. He had his hands behind his back as if he hid a weapon. He stood above them, silent, menacing.

What new terror was this? But, of course, Simon was in the plot, too, nice simple blackhearted Simon.

"Simon, what's the matter?" Antonia whispered. "Why do you look like that? What are you hiding behind your back?"

For answer Simon whipped one of his hands in front of her. From it dangled a long thick plait of silver-gold hair, pussy willow hair, limp and shining, a scarlet dahlia still tucked in its heavy strands.

Then Antonia thought she knew horror for the first time.

Strangely enough Simon's voice remained normal, his words practical. He said, "Things have been happening here by the look of it. Conroy needs a brandy. You look as if you need one, too, Tonia. And so, by God, do I."

He went to the kitchen and came back in a few moments with glasses of neat brandy. The terrible rope of hair he had tossed over the stair banisters. Antonia could scarcely move her fascinated eyes from it.

"Bella seems to have had one over the eight," he said. "I never agreed with Iris for encouraging her in that, but there you are. Iris had her way." His own eyes, small, lightless, hard, went to the lopped hair. "For the last time as far as I'm concerned," he added.

Antonia didn't take in the significance of those last words, for Dougal was on the point of collapse again.

She took a glass from Simon and made Dougal drink its contents.

"He needs a doctor to look at that head,"

291

Simon said dispassionately. "He's probably got concussion. But more probably he was meant to be dead. So he's lucky. How about Bealey? *Doctor* Bealey?"

Again Antonia had her insane desire to laugh. "You'll have to ask Henrietta for him. He's her pigeon." She sipped brandy herself and her mind began to function again. At last she could ask the question.

"Simon," she said steadily, "where's Iris?"

"Upstairs," he said vaguely. "In her room. We've just got home. You disappeared and Bealey disappeared and then Iris accidentally spilt the stuff out of her evening bag, and I saw the sleeping pills. Seven of them. Rolling over the table. The ones she'd made out you'd hidden because you might want to take an overdose. So then I had to face up to it." For a moment his mouth worked. "I wasn't that dumb. I'd wondered about several things. But when I saw how she didn't really care that her cat had got Johnnie and when I found those sleeping pills I was sure. And Bealey, of course. She's hand in glove with him."

His hands opened and shut. He turned to take the rope of shining silvery hair off the banisters.

"This is how she fooled me," he said. "Knowing I was so crazy about her. She thought I'd

292

do anything." He looked at them with his stony eyes.

"Go up and see her. You'll hardly recognise her. But it's Iris all right."

Dougal stood up.

"Just a minute. Sorry, Simon, but it's time for the police now. Gussie's disappearance has to be more fully investigated."

"I know about Gussie," Simon interrupted in his dull voice. "Or I've guessed. That was no cat screeching the other night. Yes, send for the police."

What Simon had said was true. Iris was almost unrecognisable. She had a suitcase open on the floor, and was throwing things into it. Her back was to the door and with her cropped hair and little neck above her narrow shoulders she looked like a child. Then she turned and Antonia knew that she was seeing the real Iris for the first time, the thin tight-lipped face, the suspicious eyes. With her hair shorn her one real claim to beauty had gone. There was her unadorned face, narrow, avaricious, and common.

She had been clever. Beneath her gay affectionate charming exterior one hadn't previously recognised the commonness.

"Is that you?" she said to Antonia in a hostile voice. "I'm leaving Simon as you can see.

293

I'm not staying with him another minute. The brute. Cutting off my hair like that. With my nail scissors! I thought he was going to kill me. But, no" — she gave a loud cracked laugh — "it was just the Samson and Delilah touch. Said my hair had snared him! But he needn't think he's getting away with it. I'll have him charged with assault."

The little lemon-coloured bird lay limply on the dressing-table. It might truly have been nothing but an ornament for a hat.

"And it's all your fault," she continued, throwing more clothes haphazardly into her case. "You with your passion for sleeping pills. If I hadn't found them and kept them safely in my bag you might have been dead by now. But does Simon believe that? Oh, no, he believes I intend to murder you. The great simpleton! I can't think how I came to marry him."

"Because you fancied Aunt Laura's money, perhaps," Antonia suggested.

"What! A paltry ten thousand pounds!" Iris's voice was contemptuous.

Antonia was aware that Dougal had come to stand beside her. His colour was better now, his arm firmly round her waist. All at once she was immeasurably happier. Iris with her pitiful cropped hair belonged to the nightmare of the windy house, the everlasting moan of the sea, the darkness and the rattling flaxbush, the sound of the whistling buoy that was like a trapped animal, the lost voice crying the name of a dead woman – the nightmare that was nearly over now.

"Perhaps you didn't think it so paltry at first," Dougal suggested. "It was enough for you to realise your ambition to have a place of your own after working for other people, and occasionally stealing from them, all your life. Tell me, when did Doctor Bealey first start blackmailing you? Was it the weekend you were married when you asked for a further advance of five hundred pounds?" Iris had gone very pale. Her eyes had their dangerous sparkle.

"How do you know that?"

"It's very simple to deduce. Wasn't he the Doctor Cox sentenced at the Old Bailey to five years' imprisonment for blackmail? He'd be wise to drop that doctor off his name if he plans any future crime."

"That's nothing to do with me," Iris snapped in a high-pitched voice.

"No. Except that for some reason he was able to blackmail you successfully. And I gather it isn't just because he's an ex-husband of yours. What's he got on you this time? Why is the late Miss Mildmay's money being used to buy motor-cars for crooks?"

Iris stared at him with her glittering eyes. Then suddenly she began to laugh.

"The late Miss Mildmay! That's rich, that is." She went off into another peal of laughter. "That's rich."

"You won't need all those things where you're going," came Simon's voice from the doorway. "I'd just take night things and a change of underclothing. They mightn't even let you use your own things. I don't know the customs in jails."

Iris stood rigid.

"You've got nothing on me! Just a few sleeping pills in my bag. That's not a crime."

"You shouldn't have told me it was Ptolemy screeching that night," Simon said tiredly. "I said it wasn't a cat, but you insisted it was. And you had clay on your shoes. I saw it when you came in, even though you took the precaution to have the shoes cleaned early in the morning as if Gussie had done them. You always told me lies, didn't you?"

He turned to someone in the passage. The next moment the little grey-haired woman in the neat black dress came uncertainly into the room.

"Is she here?" she asked nervously. "Is Laura here?" Her sad lost eyes went from face to face. "But I don't know these people. They're

strangers. They're not my friend, Laura Mildmay." She put her hand on Antonia's arm.
"They take me away, but I always come back
here and leave messages for Laura. Then they
lock the door and I have to call for her. She'll
miss her train, you see. She was very cross if
she missed a train."

"Who are you?" Antonia asked gently.

The old woman shook her head perplexedly.

"They say I'm Miss Rich." Suddenly she
was pointing at Iris, her face full of passionate
distress. "*She* says I am. But she's wicked!
Wicked!"

Iris's white face seemed to crack. She moved,
as if to escape that accusing finger. Suddenly
she made a dart at Simon and screamed, "It's
all your fault. If you hadn't been so sentimental
at the beginning, if you'd only let me have her
shut up...."

# XXII

"Iris has talked," Dougal said. "She said that Ralph Bealey had double-crossed her when he had asked Antonia to marry him, so now he could expect no mercy from her. This is how it was."

Dougal had a bandage round his head. Beneath it his golden eyebrows stuck in tufts, his serious blue eyes roved over the four women, Henrietta relaxed and happy in her own armchair, the shotgun propped beside her, Miss Fox sitting as stiff as a poker, her black eyes snapping, Ethel breathing heavily and still with great astonishment in the doorway, Antonia moving restlessly about, lighting one cigarette from another, her eyes never leaving Dougal's face.

"When Iris left England as a stewardess on the *Canton* she had these two women on her deck, Miss Mildmay who she could see at once hadn't long to live, and the companion, Miss Rich, who was losing her memory and being mildly silly and troublesome. Iris scented money. All her life she must have had that sort of nose. So she set herself out to be charming, ingratiating, indispensable, the inevitable result being that she left the ship at Auckland to continue her care of two helpless women.

"Then she found out about the will and about the nephew, Simon. She changed her tactics. Instead of angling for a legacy she would angle for the nephew. She persuaded Miss Mildmay to send for him. And he was easy prey to Iris's kind of woman, as you can guess."

Antonia thought of the white cat watching Simon's birds, patiently intent, sure of its final success, sure of the merciless power of its body.

"I honestly don't believe Iris had designs on Antonia's money," Dougal went on. "It had been Simon's idea that Antonia come to New Zealand and Iris, always with an eye to the main chance, thought it might be a good idea, especially if there were a lot of money. The arrival of Iris's ex-husband, who had seen her in Auckland, and, knowing Iris, had guessed she was up to something was a complete shock to her. He was too dangerous to be ignored, so all she could do was to take him into her confidence. He immediately dismissed Simon's legacy as chicken-feed. They must, through simple pliable Simon, get their hands on Antonia's large one. So they hatched up the plot on Antonia's life.

"The first attempt was made on the night of Iris and Simon's so-called honeymoon. Simon waited in Christchurch while Iris made an excuse to leave him for a couple of hours and went back to the Hilltop late, put the seaweed on the stairs and later rang up, so that Antonia would run down the stairs to answer the telephone. I don't think she expected that to succeed, it was to be a sort of curtain raiser, a good way to get Antonia into a nervous state and to work up the suicide theory.

"But at this stage things began to go wrong. Miss Rich was being difficult. She used to escape from the people who looked after her and come up to the Hilltop. She was there the night Antonia fell on the stairs, and it was she who screamed. The next day Antonia saw her. She had to be passed off as Bella's friend. It was worth Bella's while to keep silent because she was going to be allowed to have that poor devil of a husband up here and she was given the liquor for which she craved.

"Then Gussie became troublesome, he knew too much and had to be quietened. Ralph

Bealey was making proposals to Antonia behind Iris's back, and Miss Rich's final escape was publicised too widely for comfort. Yes, Iris had her hands full. But even then she didn't lose her head. She quietly carried on with her plans. The thing to do was to get rid of Antonia and then face the other problems. It was just unfortunate for her that Antonia was the kind of girl who couldn't be intimidated."

His eyes met Antonia's. Henrietta broke in excitedly.

"Oh, Dougal, isn't it wonderful! Isn't it romantic! Ethel, Miss Fox! Dougal has found the right girl at last."

With the three women beaming at him Dougal was full of angry embarrassment.

"Mother, don't be absurd! How can I marry an heiress?"

"You might ask the heiress first if she wants to marry you!" Antonia snapped. She lit another cigarette and went back to the problem. "But, Dougal, why did Gussie have to be killed? What was it he knew? And why did Miss Rich, who seems perfectly harmless, have to be hidden?"

Dougal gave an exclamation and felt in his coat pocket.

"Oh – Bella gave me something. I didn't even have time to look at it before I was hit on the head. Why, it's an old photograph. It's Miss Rich and someone else."

Antonia took the photograph from him.

"It's my mother," she said slowly. "I remember that dress she had. I was only a child. But if it's mother how can she be with this Miss Rich?"

Dougal looked over her shoulder.

"Are you sure it's Miss Rich?" he exclaimed. "Are you sure? Because I suggest it isn't. I suggest it's someone much more important."

"Dougal, don't be so legal!" Henrietta cried in an agony of impatience. "Who is the woman?"

"I suggest," said Dougal impressively, "that it's Laura Mildmay."

"Aunt Laura!" Antonia repeated. "But she's exactly like that poor woman at the Hilltop."

"Darling, don't be dumb!" Dougal was growing more excited. "Don't you see? She *is* that poor woman. She must be. It's Miss Rich, the companion, who is dead. That's the obvious explanation. No one knew the two women. It was quite safe to switch their identities. Iris and Simon have been taking a short cut to their ten thousand pounds."

"Why, good heavens!" Henrietta exclaimed. "How amazingly clever of you, Dougal. That's exactly what it must be. No wonder Antonia mustn't see the woman in case she recognised

302

her, or in case the poor thing got a little saner and remembered who she was. No wonder Iris wanted her shut up safely in an asylum."

"I suspected it all the time," Miss Fox said, tossing her neat head.

Through Antonia's head there was going a maze of thoughts: the poor lost voice in the night; the crude lipstick writing with the signature L.M. (not Gussie's message, at all); Simon saying, "Aunt Laura was good to me when I was a kid"; Ralph Bealey giving his flat cold smile; the white cat Ptolemy stalking Simon's birds; Iris covering her shorn head with a scarf, defiantly; Miss Fox calmly sitting on Ralph Bealey's chest while Henrietta stood guard with her ridiculous dangerous gun; Bella bursting into drunken tears and the woman with the gentle sad eyes begging them to find poor lost Laura. . . .

The last piece of the puzzle fitted neatly into place. She understood now why Ralph Bealey had used that device for getting into her room in Auckland. He had been investigating Iris's actions and had his suspicions as to which one of the two old women had survived. He had wanted to find something in her luggage that would give him the necessary proof. The signature on the old letter from Aunt Laura had provided it. He had somehow found out where

Iris had had the false Miss Rich sent and had obtained a specimen of her handwriting. It had provided indisputable evidence. So he had been able to telephone Iris and begin what was to have been a comparatively simple piece of blackmail. Then they had discovered the extent of Aunt Laura's fortune, and their schemes grew.

As Iris had wildly declared it was Simon who had ruined it all by being sentimental about an old woman who had once been kind to him. He wouldn't even begin the deception unless Iris promised to have Aunt Laura decently cared for. Even then, harmless as it seemed, for Aunt Laura's memory had quite gone, he didn't like it. But he was crazy about Iris. He was prepared to do almost anything to get her. In his simple way he thought it would work out. Aunt Laura couldn't use her money and no harm was being done to her.

But Iris had made the mistake of under-estimating Simon's intelligence and over-estimating her power over him. She might have known that a man who would weep over a dead bird wouldn't stand for subtle cruelty, much less murder.

Antonia saw it all as clearly as if it were being related to her, fact by fact. But beneath her shocked realisation was growing an enormous sense of relief and happiness.

"Dougal," she said slowly, "we must look after Aunt Laura. We must make this up to her with kindness. But do you see what else it means? I haven't any money at all."

"By jove, neither you have!" Dougal's jubilation was short-lived. He looked intensely worried. "I say, Miss Fox, this is going to be tricky. We've proved a will when the testatrix isn't yet deceased. What on earth is the judge going to say?"

"You worry about him tomorrow," Miss Fox said briskly. "You get your private affairs settled first.

In the doorway Ethel gave an appreciative chuckle. Dougal looked ruefully at Antonia.

"You see how it is? These women run my life. Do you mind me talking to you in front of them? You'll probably have to get used to it." He looked at her with his serious tender rueful eyes. "I haven't been much use to you. You might have been killed tonight because I was dumb enough to get knocked out. But I love you. I do love you."

"I love you, too," Antonia answered gravely.

His face lit up with its great sweetness. He bent his head to kiss her and then it was as if the three women had been spirited away, as if they were in a bare shining world alone.

305

Henrietta thumping the gun on the ground brought them back. Her heavy plain kind face was torn between joy and grief.

"Yes, that's all very well," she said. "You two can be happy. But me, I've had my hour. I don't suppose in all my life I'll ever have another chance to use this gun." Then her sense of humour returned and she smiled reminiscently. "Ah, but it was grand while it lasted."